Books by Janet Thomas
in the Linford Romance Library:

THE TIDES OF TIME
SUMMER SOJOURN
THE DANCING MAIDENS

THE OLD SUMMERHOUSE

Needing a career change, Jill Martin joins the team headed by Mark Tresidder, which is restoring the garden of Tremorran Manor in Cornwall. In a tumbledown summerhouse she stumbles upon an old diary, kept by Lady Celia Carlyon, telling of her forbidden love and shedding light on a mystery which is associated with the house. After many misunderstandings, Jill and Mark acknowledge their own love as together they solve Celia's ancient secret.

JANET THOMAS

THE OLD SUMMERHOUSE

Complete and Unabridged

LINFORD
Leicester

First published in Great Britain in 2005

First Linford Edition
published 2006

British Library CIP Data

Thomas, Janet, *1936 Oct. 24 –*
   The old summerhouse.—Large print ed.—
(Linford romance library)
   1. Historic gardens—Conservation and
restoration—England—Cornwall—Fiction
   2. Diaries—Fiction
   3. Cornwall (England)—Fiction
   4. Love stories 5. Large type books
   I. Title
   823.9′14 [F]

   ISBN 1–84617–453–8

Published by
F. A. Thorpe (Publishing)
Anstey, Leicestershire

Set by Words & Graphics Ltd.
Anstey, Leicestershire
Printed and bound in Great Britain by
T. J. International Ltd., Padstow, Cornwall

This book is printed on acid-free paper

1

Set high and surrounded on three sides by woodland, Tremorran Manor fronted the tidal river, where grassy fields sloped down to a small beach at the bottom. Built in grand style from the local granite, the house stood proudly, looking out to sea as it had done since 1778.

'Wow, just look at that! The gentry certainly knew where to build their stately homes, didn't they?'

Jill Rule turned her head to look back the way they had come. She had kicked off her shoes and was dabbling her toes in the creek, while her friend, Louise, was soaking up the sun and trying to get her first layer of tan for the year.

'Mm,' Louise replied, glancing up from the magazine she was reading. 'Whom did you say built it?'

Jill inched her way back over a ridge

of small pebbles and sat down, pulling out a leaflet from the pocket of her shorts. She tucked a lock of glossy brown hair behind one ear and folded long, slender legs beneath her.

'The first Carlyon made his fortune out of mining shares,' she read from the leaflet, 'and as his family started to climb the social ladder he had the house built to impress his neighbours.'

Louise giggled. 'Nowadays we would call it making a statement,' she said.

'That's right. Anyway, in a few generations they had become one of the country's leading families.' Jill turned back to the leaflet. 'The family died out in nineteen-fifty-five and the house was acquired by the National Trust and opened to the public.'

Louise finished the apple she had been crunching and tossed the core to a hovering gull who deftly caught it and carried if off to enjoy in a more private spot.

'This is the best holiday I've had in years,' she remarked, running a hand through her hair.

'It's the weather that's made it,' Jill replied. 'Amazing to have a mini heatwave this early. You'd never think we're still only in May, just. Someone must have known you were coming and turned it on especially.'

She rubbed her feet dry with a tissue and slipped her sandals back on.

'You are so lucky to live in Cornwall.' Louise sighed.

'It had its pros and cons, but, yes, I am.'

Jill had her hazel eyes on the deeper blue of the sea and resolved to thrust all her personal problems to the back of her mind and make the most of this glorious day.

'Are you ready to go and look around the house now?' she asked, brushing dry sand off her pink cropped trousers.

'Sure.'

Louise stretched and rose to her feet. They both collected their things together then clambered over the stile and on to the field path which led up to the house. From the top of the slope, as they looked back, the meadows which were kept grazed by a herd of docile cattle, streamed with golden buttercups all the way down to the water. Set against the azure blue of sea and sky the scene was unbelievably beautiful.

They walked down a gravelled path, where an enormous wisteria dangled its scented lilac flowers above their heads, and beneath an archway into a cobbled yard.

'I suppose you've done this guided tour before, haven't you?' Louise asked as they joined the small queue of visitors by the shallow steps which led to the front door.

'Oh, yes, several times,' Jill replied. 'The guide is a doddery old man who looks as ancient as the house, long past retirement, I should think. He reminds me of a garden gnome.'

'Oh, does he, indeed?' an amused male voice came at her elbow, and Jill whirled around to see a slim young man

4

looking down at her.

Dark eyes twinkled under heavy brows and she took in a square, determined jaw and a thatch of brown hair. He smiled, showing very white teeth in a captivating grin. He was wearing an identity label with **TOUR GUIDE** on it in large red letters.

Mortified, Jill clapped one hand to her mouth, then both she and Louise burst out laughing.

'I'm so sorry,' she said, and felt hot colour creeping up her face.

'Don't be,' the guide said, shaking his head. 'You were right. Jim retired at the end of last season. I'm Mark — Mark Tresidder,' he added and held out a hand.

'Jill Martin, and my friend Louise Harris.'

His clasp was firm and warm as he took her hand, and when Jill looked up and met his lively brown eyes she felt the sudden tug of this man's charisma and knew that he was a person she would not forget in a hurry.

'Dishy!' Louise murmured out of his hearing, as Mark led the party over the worn stone threshold and into the house. Jill nodded but did not feel inclined to discuss him further. It seemed somehow disloyal, although why she should feel like that about a man she had scarcely met, she had no idea.

They were climbing a flight of granite stairs now, where a lattice-paned window afforded a glimpse of the magnificent gardens which were at the height of their springtime splendour. Towering bushes of brilliant rhododendrons, camellias and magnolias filled the vista with colour, and were complemented by the emerald green of the newly-cut lawns. Flower beds full of bright tulips and forget-me-nots fringed the grass, while in the distance the woodland was a haze of new green and the soft mist of bluebells.

'We are now entering the Long Gallery,' Mark Tresidder was saying, 'which, as you can see, is hung with the collection of flower paintings executed by Lady Celia Carlyon in eighteen-ninety-eight.'

He paused and looked directly at Jill, giving her that heart-stopping smile again.

'According to the printed guide to the house, which you may have read,' he went on, 'there is said to be an intriguing secret attached to these paintings. They are reputed to have some hidden meaning, and so far nobody has managed to find the key to this mystery and discover what it is. So we can only admire them for their exquisite artistry and wonder about their origin.'

'They really are exquisite. He wasn't exaggerating.' Louise was gazing transfixed at the delicate water-colours. 'Look at these roses — you can almost smell them.'

'I know. I can never get enough of the pictures,' Jill replied. 'I've seen them time and time again but they always seem to be so fresh and new. Lady

Celia was a fantastic artist. There are more of her pictures around the house, landscapes and so on, which are pretty good, too, but they're not a patch on her flowers. In the other room are a lot more paintings of exotic plants from other countries, but I like these simple ones best.'

She looked back over her shoulder, alerted by the sudden quietness of the room, then called out, 'Louise, come on, we're getting left behind!'

The two girls ran across the vast expanse of patterned carpet and caught up with the rest just as Mark Tresidder was saying, 'We now pass down this corridor on the right to the wing where the bedrooms are situated.'

Bringing up the rear, the girls joined the party as they followed their guide down the wood-panelled passage which was decorated with hanging tapestries, their colours still as jewel-bright as when they were woven hundreds of years before.

'The door on the left leads to what

was Lady Celia's room.'

Mark indicated a closed door with a notice on it saying, **No Admittance**.

'Unfortunately it's in a state of disrepair at the moment and I'm afraid that we can't go in there today. A storm last winter brought down some slates from the roof and rain water leaked in causing quite extensive damage.'

'Oh, that's disappointing,' Louise murmured. 'I'd like to have seen that room. I wonder if that's where she did her painting.'

'A good excuse to have another holiday soon.' Jill smiled. 'You'll have to come back when it's been repaired, and finish the tour.'

Later, back at the tiny cottage that was Jill's pride and joy, the two were lingering over the remains of a meal when Louise spoke as she stirred the spoon round and round her coffee cup.

'Have you had any further thoughts as to what you're going to do now that you're out of a job, Jill?'

Jill winced. Put like that it sounded

catastrophic, but Louise had never been one to beat around the bush. They had met ten years ago at teachers' training college and had been firm friends ever since. Louise's practical commonsense always made a foil for Jill's more dreamy and imaginative character, and was now forcing her to face up to the unpleasant truth.

'Only that I'm not going back to teaching,' Jill replied, nibbling thoughtfully at a biscuit.

Her elbows on the table, she gazed unseeingly out of the window at the courtyard which was bright with tubs of flowers.

'Understandably.' Louise nodded.

'I've got some savings which will buy me time to think about it and look around before I decide,' Jill added. 'Thank goodness, I've paid off the bulk of the mortgage on this place. I bless Gran for her legacy there.'

'I should think so,' Louise said, looking through the trees at the sparkle of water just visible through their thick foliage. 'Imagine what a place like this would cost at today's prices! An idyllic cottage, part of an old estate, overlooking the creek, no less. You're sitting on a gold mine, girl.'

Jill chuckled and nodded.

'It came to me at just the right time,' she said, 'so I could rent it out while I was away. That's where the savings came from, Lou. I couldn't save a penny when I was at college, or teaching in London, as you can imagine.'

She turned back into the room and looked around her home fondly. This was her haven which had seen her through the miserable time of her illness almost twelve months ago.

'Something inside me still resents the fact that the kids seem to have won though,' she muttered, and Louise reached out a sympathetic hand across the table.

'It wasn't like that, Jill. It was only because you weren't well that it felt that way. You didn't realise yourself how stressed you were and neither did anyone else.'

'It was the way everything happened at once, I suppose, because as well as breaking up with Max, of course, there was Mum still depending on me so much, although it had been two years since Dad died.'

She gave a sigh and poured more coffee into her cup.

'With Max and me, I think we both realised that our time together had come to a natural end. We just weren't right for each other, but the timing couldn't have been worse, just when I'd agreed to take on those extra classes because there was a shortage of supply teachers. I felt sure I could cope with everything.' She sighed. 'More fool me!'

Jill replaced her cup on its saucer and passed a hand across her face.

'That's what made the discipline problems so much worse, Lou. In the normal way, I could have handled those troublemakers with my eyes shut, no problem, but as you know it all got on top of me in the end and . . . ' Jill shrugged and opened her palms expressively.

'Of course it did,' Louise sympathised. 'I was only surprised it hadn't happened sooner. I know only too well what it is to face a class of stroppy teenagers. I admire you for coping as long as you did.'

'Well, anyway, I've thrown in the towel now, let's face it.'

Jill straightened and slapped the flat of her hand on the table top in a show of determination.

'Time for a career change, time to be positive, time for action, not words.' Then catching Louise's eye she said with a mischievous grin, 'Actually, I was lying to you just now. I have had an idea.'

'You have?' Louise leaned forward with interest brightening her face. 'What's that?'

Jill edged a shade closer. 'Well, when we went to Tremorran the other day, I saw a notice in the window where we bought our guided tour tickets, which said they were embarking on a big project in the woodland behind the house. Apparently there's a very neglected area down there which was abandoned years ago when there weren't enough gardeners to keep it going. Now the National Trust wants to restore it and they're taking on extra staff. I thought I might apply.'

'Really?' Louise's brows rose. 'Well, I know how much you love gardening, Jill.'

She glanced out of the window towards the neat grass and colourful flowerbeds at the front of the house.

'But this sounds like hard graft to me. Do you think you're up to it?'

'Actually, I feel that it's exactly right for me as things are at the moment. I should imagine it will be fairly undemanding on the brain, wouldn't you? Exercise and the open air — I shall love it. And right on my doorstep, Louise. It seems meant for me, don't you think? And as well, it'll be so tiring that I won't lie awake at night going over the past, you see.' She grinned. 'That's what I'm hoping anyway.'

'Well, in that case, I wish you all the luck in the world. Seriously, I'm glad you've got such a positive plan, because I was a bit worried about going back tomorrow and leaving you on your own again.'

Her friend gave Jill an anxious look.

'Lou, it's been fantastic having you here, I can't tell you how much I've enjoyed your company.' Jill squeezed her hand. 'But truly, I am better now and I'm really looking forward to getting on with the next stage of my life.'

★ ★ ★

The interview was over and Jill was delighted at having been offered a job as one of the team, but before her new life took over and her time became no longer her own, there was something she still had to do. Jill could no longer

15

put off the fact that it had been too long since she had been to see her mother. Since Louise's visit, which had lasted a fortnight, the time had absolutely flown as she tended her own garden, sent in her application form and waited to be called for the interview. Now that was all behind her and she could prevaricate no longer.

A meeting with her mother was not something which Jill was looking forward to. They were as different as chalk and cheese and had never been exactly close, although Laura had clung desperately to her daughter for a while after Jill's father had died. There had been frequent phone calls between them, and although phone calls were all very well, Jill knew where her duty lay and would rather go of her own accord than wait to be summoned. So she set out for Malpas and her mother's hillside bungalow.

'Lovely to see you dear,' her mother greeted her, kissing the air somewhere around Jill's cheek, and ushered her inside in a cloud of expensive perfume.

Impeccably made up, with not a hair out of place, Laura always had the effect on her daughter of making her feel like a street urchin, and she glanced ruefully at her jeans and old shirt as she replied.

'Hello, Mum, how are you?'

She followed Laura into the sitting-room which overlooked the tidal reaches of the River Fal and took a seat in the bay window. Laura sank down into a velvet-covered armchair beside her and patted her hair.

'Oh, not too bad, rushed off my feet as usual. There's the Women's Institute monthly meeting coming up and I have to bake for that and the Friends of the Hospital are having a fund-raising bazaar and I'm doing a stall for them. Then there's the charity shop. I still work there two mornings a week.'

Nothing changes, Jill thought. Laura was the typical committee woman and charity worker and revelled in it, although she never ceased to complain about the amount of time it entailed. With a flash of insight, Jill realised that all this activity now filled her mother's otherwise empty life and that she was actually more dependent on the charitable causes than they were upon her, and felt a twinge of compassion.

Laura's voice had run its course and she was saying at last, 'Well, now tell me all your news. You are still determined on this gardening thing, I suppose. A bit of a come-down from teaching after all the years you spent training for a career, isn't it? I should have thought that now you're better . . . '

'Mum, I need a complete change, and you know how I've always loved the out-of-doors. It's going to be very exciting, especially not knowing what we're going to find.'

'I was really disappointed when you broke up with Max.' Laura gave her daughter a disapproving look. 'He sounded a very sensible young man, just the sort you needed.'

Jill scowled. 'It takes two people to

make a relationship work, Mum. This one had run its course.'

'Hmm,' Laura said through pursed lips and drummed her fingers on the arm of her chair. 'Well, I'll go and make us a cup of tea.'

She rose and Jill followed her into the tiny, spotless kitchen. When she been a child, they had lived in the country, in an old, converted barn which she had loved. The kitchen then had been the hub of the house, with a warm and welcoming Aga around which they all congregated in winter.

She recalled with a rush of nostalgia how she and her younger brother had spent entire days when they were out of school roaming the fields and woods. It had given them both a love of the out-of-doors which had remained with them ever since. Torn between this love and the practicality of earning a living, as Jill grew older she had taken her mother's advice and gone in for teaching, but now she was perfectly capable of deciding the next move for herself.

'I'm really glad I can stay in Cornwall, Mum,' she said with feeling, as she leaned on the window-sill and glanced out at the sparkling river.

Laura was setting a tray with an embroidered cloth and putting out dainty cups and saucers. Jill thought of the cheap and cheerful mugs which were all that she ever used herself, and smiled inwardly.

Back in the sitting-room, she sipped her tea and reached for a home-made cookie as she asked, 'Have you heard from Tim lately?'

Her mother crossed elegant legs and placed her cup and saucer on the low table nearby.

'Not for a couple of months, but you know what your brother's like. If he's not mapping out the haunts of the lesser-spotted doodlebug or some other obscure creature, he's got his head buried in books about it.'

Jill laughed out loud at this accurate description of her academic brother, who worked for the local nature trust and was heavily involved in all things ecological.

'I tell him that it's high time he found himself a nice girl and settled down, but it's like water off a duck's back.'

'Or a doodlebug's,' Jill replied with a grin and they shared a rare moment of togetherness.

★ ★ ★

'Oh, hello, again!' When she turned up for her new job at Tremorran, Jill was surprised to find that Mark Tresidder seemed to be in charge of the group assembling in the area at the back of the house where they had been told to meet.

'Hi — um — Jill, of course, isn't it?'

She nodded.

'I didn't realise that you were to be my boss,' she said with a smile. 'Garden restoration doesn't seem compatible somehow with being a tour guide.'

Mark laughed.

'This is my real job,' he replied. 'I only help out indoors at weekends.'

He ran a hand through his springy hair and looked down at the papers he was holding in the other.

'Well, everybody should be here by now,' he said, glancing at his watch. 'So let's get started.'

He jumped nimbly up on to a broken brick wall and raised his voice.

'Hello, everybody. I'm Mark and I shall soon get to know your names as we go along. We're standing now in what was the stable-yard. I'm sure you remember from the plan you were all given that this door behind me leads into the walled garden, where herbs and vegetables for the kitchen would have been grown. There were several hot-houses as well, full of tropical fruits, I suppose, and also rare and exotic plants from around the world.'

'It takes a bit of imagining now,' Jill remarked, standing on tip-toe to peer over the wall.

She could see one end of a tumbled, wooden frame, completely glassless, green with mould and all but buried in a riot of brambles and nettles.

Mark nodded.

'Uh-huh. As you can see, it's going to be quite a challenge. Out there are thirty acres of overgrown woods, shrubberies, streams and a lake, plus a maze, a grotto, ornamental terraces and formal gardens, all buried.'

'And just six of us? You must be joking,' a surly voice growled, and a huge, beefy man built like a navvy removed a cigarette end from his mouth and ground it into the mossy cobbles with the heel of his heavy boot.

'Sorry — Steve, isn't it? I should have explained,' Mark called back. 'You people are the hard core of paid workers. We shall also have back-up from a regular supply of volunteers, students, retired locals, weekend-helpers. There's quite a bit of interest in this project, and we shall get people on working holidays which are organised by the environmental groups. They'll all be a great help.'

He jumped down from the wall.

'I guess that's long enough standing around. Let's do some real work.'

He walked towards the door of an old stable which had been repaired and fitted with a new lock.

'Our tools are kept in here. I have to count them all out to you and count them back in each day as we finish.'

He disappeared inside the building and emerged with his arms full.

'We'll start by clearing the main paths so we can find our way around. The whole area will have to be hand cleared first.'

'That's because if you bring in the heavy machinery too soon you could damage what's underneath, is it?' a thin young man called Rob asked.

'Right. We have to do it the hard way first, then see what structures we find and if they're worth restoring, also which, if any, of the original plants have survived.'

'It sounds quite exciting, like searching for buried treasure,' Jill said.

'More like hacking a way into Sleeping Beauty's castle,' Megan Williams added with a grin.

Jill liked Megan already. Dark haired and bubbly, she always seemed to have a smile on her face.

'Now, will each of you take something. There are secateurs, bill-hooks, shears, loppers — take what you can handle best, plus gloves. Don't try any of the macho stuff. There are thorns in there three inches long. Oh, and take a couple of wheelbarrows. There'll be a dumper truck here soon. We can come to and fro with the stuff as we cut it.'

He locked the door again and they all set off.

'This way. We'll work in a team today on the main pathways. I'll be backing you up with the chain-saw, so shout when you come across any fallen trees or overhanging branches.'

He laid the saw down temporarily, picked up a bill-hook and started work alongside Jill and Meg who were wielding shears and loppers against the dense tangle of dead bracken, brambles and nettles which reared in places high above their heads.

'First we need the sides cutting back just enough to find the way through,' Mark said, slashing at the overhanging vegetation with a long arm.

'Well, it would be good if you stick to the overhead clearance like that,' Meg said, 'then we two shorties can do a side each.'

'Good thinking,' Jill said and for a while they all hacked and chopped companionably.

The dry, dead stuff came away easily and they raked it into piles for loading on the return trip.

'We'll have our work cut out to get all this old stuff cleared before the new growth really starts sprouting,' Mark said as he raked a heap of debris to the side of the path. 'I wanted to get started on it months ago but all the red tape took so long to sort out that it didn't happen that way.'

He hacked vigorously at a clump of brambles. His thick brown hair was sprinkled with bits of leaves and twigs and he shook himself like a dog to clear it. Jill wanted to laugh but something in Mark's intense and somehow forbidding expression stopped her. She looked at him with interest, wondering what it was about him that intrigued her. He seemed to be a mixture of authority and defensiveness.

'Phew, let's take a breather, shall we? This sort of thing is better done in short bursts,' Mark said and propped his bill-hook against a tree then subsided on to a fallen log, moving his long legs up to make room for the two girls.

'Where are you from, Mark?' Jill asked, discarding her jacket.

The physical exercise had warmed her and now the sun was out as well, peering through the newly-cut canopy and shining into places that had not felt its warmth for years.

'I'm local but I lived in south-west London for several years while I was doing research at Kew,' he replied. 'But I needed to be with my family, and to earn some money as well. This job seemed to be the ideal answer to both.'

His dark eyes were unsmiling and his jaw set as he gazed into the middle distance and Jill wondered idly why he didn't lighten up a bit more. Mark shifted into a more comfortable position and went on.

'I really want to make a career in forestry, woodland management, something like that, eventually. How about you, Meg?'

'Oh, any outdoor job suits me,' she replied cheerfully. 'I just couldn't stand to work in an office. I'm picking daffodils at the weekends as well, over at the flower farm. I fancied coming to Cornwall to keep my gran company. We've always been close but now she can't travel as she's not very well, so I don't see her often.'

Mark nodded, then turned away.

'And you, Jill?' he asked.

'Oh, I've loved gardens and gardening since I was a little tot,' she replied. 'Once I thought I might make a career out of market gardening, or running a nursery or something, but instead, I went into teaching. I needed some reliable money before I could follow the dream.'

His eyes stayed on her face as Jill shifted position on the less than comfortable seat and went on softly.

'There are personal reasons as well why I applied for this particular job.'

She put a hand to her hair wondering why she was feeling so dishevelled, and discovered that she had lost her tie-back in the bushes. She shoved her hair behind her ears and met Mark's eyes as he questioned her with a lift of an eyebrow.

'Oh? Can we ask what they are, or is it private?'

'Well, it's a long story, really.'

Mark glanced at his watch. 'We can spare a few more minutes. We've been doing really well so far and we'll have plenty to show Richard when he turns up this afternoon.'

Jill recalled the pleasant, middle-aged man who had interviewed them and said, 'OK then. You see, my great-great-grandfather was head gardener on this estate when the manor house was occupied.'

2

'Here?' Mark and Meg chorused together, both their faces a picture of astonishment. 'Wow, no wonder you're keen on helping restore it,' Meg said, her black eyes shining with interest. 'How many years ago was that?'

'Oh, he started as a gardener's boy somewhere around 1892 I should say. He was born in 1880. He worked his way up. So he'd be here just over a hundred years ago in that case. Actually, he was the last gardener they had. The Carlyon family died out while he was still employed here, although I think he was kept on as a sort of caretaker-cum-gardener for a few years after that. Then during the war, the house was run as a convalescent home for soldiers, then it was left empty for years until the Trust took it over.'

'So that's why the grounds have got

into this state,' Meg remarked.

'It's a bit eerie to think that the last time they were tended, great-great-grandfather Martin was in charge,' Jill said dreamily, staring into space. 'I should think he had an interesting life actually because when he was still a young man, he was sent abroad by Sir Charles Carlyon to search for rare plants. His name is mentioned in the guide book.'

'Oh, yes, that was the fashionable thing in the Victorian age,' Mark said, 'to collect exotic species. It led to a lot of one-upmanship, I think, as each family tried to grow something that no-one else had.'

'What happened to him then?' Meg asked.

'I don't really know,' Jill replied with a shake of her head, 'only that he was killed in the war in 1915, leaving his wife with two sons and four daughters to bring up on her own.' She shrugged. 'Our family history is a bit sketchy, and I've never got around to finding out more. I think he must have travelled a lot before he died, probably on more plant-hunting trips. I remember my grandfather had a cabinet of curios from around the world, which had come down to them from his grandfather, and which I was allowed to play with as a special treat when I was a little girl.'

Her gaze wandered to the big house whose roof was just visible between the trees. Glimpses of water came and went as the branches moved in the wind, and the blue eye of the creek seemed to be winking at her. The house itself didn't seem to have changed much with the passage of time. There were no additions built on to the original structure, and now that it was a listed building it would stay that way.

It was easy to imagine it as it must have been in its hey-day, she thought, picturing the lay-out of the house in her mind. The oval drive in the front was still there, where the county families had swept up in their carriages, visiting for parties and balls, soirees and musical evenings . . .

'Right, time to get back to it, I think.'

Mark slapped his hands on his knees and Jill jerked out of her reverie and rose to her feet with the rest of them.

For a long time they hacked and snipped, wading farther into the overgrown wilderness until Jill's shears snagged against something hard and unyielding. When she laid them down and pushed aside the brambles and clinging tendrils of ivy she discovered a tumbled wall.

'Mark,' she called over her shoulder, 'there's something here. Look,' she added pointing a finger as he pushed his way through the knee-high undergrowth to join her, 'it could be part of a building.'

'Oh, that's interesting.'

Mark lifted another curtain of vegetation. 'It goes on, look, around the corner.'

He dropped his tools and fished in a pocket.

'Let's have a look at this old plan of the house.'

He spread the paper out on a newly-cut tree stump.

'Mm. We came down this track here,' he said and traced it with a forefinger, 'so now we must be about here. Yes! Look, there was a summerhouse there, in just about the right spot.'

He raised his head and his eyes met Jill's. They were both kneeling, their heads very close together as they studied the plan. The others were some distance away and the two of them could have been the only people in the wood. It was very quiet in this secluded place, apart from the hum of insects around them and the sound of birdsong. In such close proximity, Jill could feel the heat emanating from Mark's body. To her annoyance, she felt her heartbeat quickening at the purely animal attraction of this man, and to break the tension which continued to build she said inanely, echoing his remarks, 'A summerhouse? Oh, isn't that interesting?'

'Yes,' Mark's terse reply came, and Jill was sure he had been aware of it, too. As he jumped to his feet she added, 'I wonder how much of it's left.'

'We'll soon see.' Mark folded up the plan. 'We'll get everybody on to it and find out.'

He shouted for the others to join them.

Half an hour's concerted effort by the whole team eventually revealed the remains of the structure. Considering its age and the degree of neglect it had suffered, it was surprisingly recognisable. The gabled façade with its triple-arched entrance was still intact.

A huge sycamore tree had fallen through the roof at some time and flattened both it and one of the walls. The others were still standing and the interior was full of slates from the roof and weeds that had grown up through the cobbled floor.

There were some remnants of furniture as well, two broken cane chairs, a small cupboard leaning drunkenly in one corner, warped and green with moss, and what might have been a card table, made of cane like the chairs. A stone bench fixed to the back wall must once have looked out upon a beautiful vista, now nothing but a wilderness.

'It must have been a lovely retreat for someone in its day,' Jill remarked as they surveyed the results of their work. 'It's a very attractive building.'

'This is where the pleasure grounds were, according to the map,' Mark replied, 'with the summerhouse as part of the whole thing. Nearby there was a rose garden with a big tree in the middle, and a lawn with a stream at the bottom of it, running down to the creek. There was a grotto near here somewhere, too, and a sundial.'

'In Xanadu did Kubla Khan a stately pleasure dome decree,' Jill murmured under her breath.

'What was that?' Megan asked with a quizzical look on her face.

'Oh, just a poem I remember from

school,' Jill said lightly, skipping some of the lines to go on. 'So twice five miles of fertile ground with lawns and bowers were girded round. And there were gardens bright with sinuous rills . . . '

Then to her amazement, Mark added the rest, their eyes locking as he went on, 'Where blossomed many an incense-bearing tree.'

'You know it!' Jill exclaimed in delight.

'Coleridge, yes?' he said with a grin and Jill nodded, smiling back as she savoured this unexpected meeting of minds.

'I always enjoyed poetry lessons.'

Mark's eyes stayed on hers for a moment, warmer and softer than she had seen them before. Practical Megan brought them back to the present.

'Well, there's a flat area over there which doesn't seem quite as overgrown as the rest. Perhaps that's where the lawn was. There aren't so many big trees, only the smaller self-sown ones.

Look.' They followed her pointing finger.

'You're right,' Mark said. 'Let's go and have a look.'

Jill stayed behind for a moment, looking around the little room, wondering about the person or people who had made this their retreat. The atmosphere was so peaceful and quiet now that the others had moved off that she could picture it as it must have been in those long-ago days, when ladies — she had a hunch that it had been a woman, or women who had used it — had the leisure to sit through the drowsy, summer afternoons with their tapestry or books, in this heavenly place.

Jill shook herself back to the present and, full of curiosity, moved to open the cupboard doors to find dust, mouse droppings and bits of chewed paper. She closed them quickly and tried the two warped and twisted drawers above. One of the rusted knobs came off in her hand and the other one seemed to be stuck fast. Jill gave it a sharp tug, then recoiled as the drawer came right out and she was sent staggering backwards.

She recovered her balance and moved to replace it, but as she did so she caught sight of something which had slipped down behind the back of the drawer into the casing. Jill bent down for a closer look. More dust, but there was actually something down there as well.

Gingerly, she put in a hand, testing for spiders of which she was terrified, and to her amazement retrieved a crumbling book. It reeked of damp and its marbled cover was stained with mildew, but nevertheless she could open it with care. Then came another surprise. Its pages were covered with handwriting, old, spidery, copperplate handwriting. Jill lifted one or two of the corners, afraid of tearing it, or that it might crumble to bits in her hand, and felt a flip of excitement. She seemed to have stumbled across somebody's diary, and a very ancient one, too.

At the sound of voices coming back,

Jill hastily picked up the drawer to replace it and discovered that out of it had fallen a splintered pen with a rusty nib, also a glass ink bottle, its inside stained black with long-dried ink. So someone had sat here, writing her diary, probably in secret, else why should she have kept it in the summerhouse? Jill felt a surge of excitement and slipped the book into the pocket of her discarded jacket. She didn't want to show it to anyone at the moment, not until she had had a chance to look at it herself.

'What a lovely old magnolia tree that is,' Megan was saying, looking over her shoulder. 'Amazing how it's survived for so long, really.'

Jill caught up on the conversation and looked across to where they had come from. There was a sort of clearing there as Megan had said, and in the middle, thrusting its head up through the tangled vegetation around it, was a huge pink magnolia, still flowering bravely against all the odds.

'Is that the tree on the plans?' Jill asked, catching a dropping petal in her hand and stroking the cool perfection of it. Mark nodded.

'Seems like it,' he said. 'It's in the right place. All signs of the rose bushes have disappeared, of course, but look at the size of that trunk. Stands to reason that it must have been there a long time.'

'Wow, it must be really hardy,' Jill replied, and Mark added, 'But as they come from the eastern Himalayas where they grow naturally in the wild, perhaps it's not too surprising.'

'Anyway, now that we've found it, we can look after the poor thing and reward it for all its years of struggling,' Megan said.

'You sound as if you want to wrap it up in blankets and coddle it with chicken soup!' Mark said as he threw back his head and laughed.

The laughter was infectious and soon they had all joined in. Jill was thinking to herself what a different person this intriguing man was when he let himself go and forgot for a moment whatever demons were tormenting him.

It was late in the evening by the time Jill had returned home. She placed the diary in the airing cupboard to dry out while she had a shower and washed the debris out of her hair. Maybe by the time she had cooked and eaten a meal as well, the book would be in a better condition for handling. Then at last she could really see what it contained.

Much later, and with a cup of coffee at her elbow, Jill placed the diary on a small table in front of her. It was about the size of an old-fashioned ledger and had leather-bound corners just like one. She eased open the first page. There was a name there, faint but just decipherable. *Celia Carlyon*, she read, *aged twenty*.

'Wow!' Jill exclaimed aloud, for Celia Carlyon had been the young woman whose flower paintings still adorned the walls of her former home.

There was a date next, April 4, 1901,

the year in which Queen Victoria had died. Jill remembered that much from school history lessons. What a landmark in time that had been — the end of the Victorian age. Jill tried to imagine what Celia's life would have been like.

It had been an incredibly different way of life then. Everyone knew their place and deferred to their superiors, accepting their lot without question. To the ordinary, working-class person, a young woman of Celia's position, titled, rich and privileged, must have had an enviable existence, and living in Tremorran Manor must have seemed like paradise.

Jill scanned the page again and was soon lost in Celia's story of so long ago. Told in her own words, it sprang from the page as fresh as if it were happening in front of her eyes at that moment, and Jill became deaf both to the ringing of her phone and the crying of her hungry cat as the past reached out and enfolded her.

'Oh, darling Papa, say yes, please!'

The echo of Celia's voice came down the years as Jill followed the faded handwriting with a finger.

I just had to get it settled today. I could not bear to wait any longer for him to make up his mind. The spring sunshine has been getting stronger every day this week and it is time to start on the work if I am ever to realise my heart's desire. So I kneeled on the hearth-rug and looked up into Papa's face, willing him to give in. Then I put on my little-girl look which I know he can't resist and tipped my head to one side. I smiled to myself when I noticed him falter and look away into the fire. He was weakening!

Jill smiled as well at the image of the spirited girl her words conjured up, and she read on, entranced.

'But hacking out a garden, child,' Father said. *'Think what it would do to your hands, your fingernails!'*

As if I care a fig about fingernails, Celia wrote. *He picked up one of my hands and ran a finger over it as if it* were already roughened from hard labour.

'You're a young lady, Celia, not some common working woman who has to help feed her family by growing vegetables. What your poor, dead mother would have to say at the way you've turned out, I can't imagine.'

He stroked his bushy whiskers and looked bewildered. As his only child I know he thinks me headstrong and wilful and sometimes wishes that I'd been born a boy. Oh, so do I! Then I jumped to my feet and straightened my skirt. I'd put on my navy-blue poplin and my high-necked, tucked and frilled blouse with its leg-of-mutton sleeves fastened with tiny buttons, trying to look as demure as any father could wish. Then I perched myself on the arm of Papa's chair and slipped an arm through his.

'She would say I'm a credit to you,' I replied, dropping a kiss on his forehead. 'It's a new century now, Papa, and soon we'll have a new king and queen. Times are changing.'

I jumped up and rested one finger on the low cane tables as I did a twirl around it as if it were a parasol, but he did not even smile.

'But gardening,' he growled like a bear. 'Celia, it's just not ladylike behaviour.'

And he glared at me as only Papa can.

Jill chuckled to herself. Celia's writing was so descriptive that she could picture the scene as if it were being acted out in front of her. How lovely that she had liked gardening. Jill felt a tenuous bond forming between her and this spirited young lady who had obviously to fight for what she wanted and had been determined to get her own way against all the odds. She squinted over the faded lettering and held it closer to the light to read more of Celia's story, in the girl's own words.

'Oh Papa, be reasonable,' I said and pouted my lips prettily. 'Lots of women like creating beautiful gardens. Look at Miss Jekyll.'

But he heaved himself out of his chair and stamped around the room in annoyance and I clapped one hand to my mouth in dismay as I wondered if I might have gone too far this time.

This time, Jill thought with a chuckle as she raised her head from the page. It sounds as if Celia was well used to fighting her corner. Oh, well done, Celia, she thought, you were a girl born out of your time. You sound like a thoroughly modern young woman, standing up for what you believe in.

'Celia,' Father had said, 'I've heard enough about Gertrude Jekyll to last me a lifetime. Just because she's happy enough to potter around in tweeds and sensible boots, grubbing in the soil, doesn't mean that it's what I want for you.'

So with a bent head and a quiet sob that I felt sure he would not be able to resist I said imploringly then, 'Don't you want me to be happy, too, Papa?' I think he must have expected a mouthful of defiance from me, because it seemed to catch him completely off-guard, just as I had hoped!

'Oh, child.' His arms went round me in a hug. 'Of course I do.'

He looked totally bewildered and I felt slightly sorry for being such a bother to him as he shook his head sadly. Inwardly, I was seething at having to sink to such cajolery in order to get my own way. Why should a woman have to fight for every little bit of freedom, whereas a boy can do more or less whatever he wants? It is so unfair. However if cajolery was what it took, that was how it would have to be, so I hardened my heart and waited. And at last he spoke the words I wanted to hear, although somewhat grudgingly.

'I suppose so . . . oh, I suppose it will be all right.'

My heart flipped over in excitement. At last! I could afford to be generous now that he had given in, so I flung my arms around his neck and dropped a kiss on his cheek.

'Oh, Papa, thank you!' I said. 'You won't regret this, I promise. I'll do one of my flower paintings for you tonight. You'd like that, wouldn't you?'

Oh, I love Papa dearly, but he can be so stubborn sometimes.

Jill came to the end of a page and rubbed her aching eyes. But there was no way she was going to put the book down yet, it was far too fascinating. She read on . . .

I slipped upstairs to change out of my smart skirt and into something more fitting for the out-of-doors, Celia went on as Jill turned the page, and on the way I glanced out of the landing window. Although it is only early April the lawns are a lush green now and the rhododendron bushes edging the carriage drive are brilliant with flowers. I slipped on my comfortable old brown wool skirt and a warm jacket, then went outside into the sunshine. I see that the daffodil bulbs in the beds below the terrace, which started showing their sturdy tips before Christmas, are bursting into flower. I passed them as I crossed the lawn into the walled garden and slipped through the far door which leads to the dell. The door is festooned with ivy and never used now by anyone except me. The dell is terribly overgrown and has been neglected since we children grew up and there is no-one to play in it any more. But now that I have Papa's permission, I plan to transform it into my own private garden!

It had been a wonderful playground for me and the cousins when we were small. In fact, I noticed that the rotting ropes of the old swing are still hanging from the magnolia tree. I can remember when Edward and Julian built a tree-house up there and then vowed to spend the night in it. They stuck it out until about eleven o'clock, when the hoot of an owl and the ghostly shadows terrified them so, that they crept back into the house and their own beds, hoping nobody would notice!

The summerhouse is still there, too, under the branches of the magnolia, *but of course it is half-buried with brambles and nettles. I want all that cleared away before I start on the garden. I shall get William to help me. It will be a perfect reason for us to be together and altogether proper! Beside it I shall have rose-beds and a lawn. Oh, I am so bursting with ideas that my head is aching. I think that I shall go to bed now.*

'Oh, so must I,' Jill said aloud, coming out of the past and back to the present day.

She glanced at the clock and stared in surprise. It was almost midnight! She had been so sunk in the past that the evening had flown by unheeded. Reluctantly she slipped the book into a drawer and rose to her feet, yawning and stretching.

She would come back to it at the earliest opportunity. Next day, however, she had promised to go over to have lunch with her mother and Tim, her brother. Jill begrudged the time, but a promise was a promise and there was no way she could slide out of it now. Besides she was looking forward to a chat with her brother, whom she hadn't seen for a long time.

★   ★   ★

'So, how are things with you, Tim?' Jill enquired as they lounged, after a lovely meal and wine, in Laura's comfortable, deep armchairs. 'And what project are you working on at the moment?'

Their mother had gone to call on an elderly friend next door and they were temporarily alone in the house.

'It seems ages since we've had a face-to-face talk.'

'It is ages, and you know how I hate the phone for chatting. It's just not the same. You miss so much by not being able to see someone's face.'

Tim ran a hand through his shock of thick fair hair and grinned at his sister through heavy spectacles.

'I've been meaning for ages to come over and see you, but I've been so busy lately that the time just hasn't been there. But I will, soon. And you're sure that you're really recovered now?'

'Yes, I really am,' Jill replied. 'This job is just what I needed, undemanding, plenty of healthy fresh air and no responsibilities. I'm really enjoying it. And I'll look forward to your visit. Better give me a ring first to make sure I'm in. I haven't got an answer-phone,' she added with a grin, knowing her brother hated them!

'Let's go out for a walk. I need exercise after that huge lunch and it'll do you good, too,' Tim said with authority.

He uncrossed his long legs and rose to his feet. Tim was a big man in every way. Tall and broad-shouldered, with a head of leonine hair on a thick neck, he resembled an all-in wrestler rather than the naturalist and academic which he was. He was a total extrovert, with a big voice and a loud laugh and even his gestures were expansive.

'I know that makes sense,' Jill said,

'but I'm really comfortable at the moment.'

Then she glanced at her brother and saw the determined look in his eyes.

'Oh, all right then,' she replied with a sigh, 'but only a short one, not one of your muddy hikes, mind.'

'Would a sedate stroll along by the river suit you, my lady?'

Tim's blue eyes twinkled as he held out both hands and hauled her to her feet, then crooked an arm towards her. Jill slipped her hand into it with a giggle. They had always got on well together although Tim was four years older than she was.

As they wandered along the edge of the creek, beneath the leafy trees, and watched the water-fowl on the mud-flats of the tidal river, Tim said, turning to her, 'You were telling me about this new job of yours. You did say that they are taking on volunteer helpers, didn't you?'

'Yes, I did. Why?'

'Well, I need a break.'

He paused and leaned on the wooden fence beside her.

'We've just come to the end of a long period of research into all sorts of complicated things that I won't bore you with, and I was wondering if I might come along. What do you think?'

'Oh, Tim, that would be brilliant!' Jill's face lit up with enthusiasm. 'We need all the help we can get. That jungle just has to be seen to be believed. It looks like it goes on for ever.'

'It sounds interesting. It occurred to me that there may be plants in there which, if not exactly rare, might be a bit out of the ordinary, you know? Perhaps species which have hybridised over all the years of neglect and become something new.'

Her brother's eyes glowed at the prospect.

'Wishful thinking,' Jill retorted, and Tim's face fell. 'All you're likely to find is rhododendrons twenty feet high and every special species of bramble and nettle in the known world, and I speak from experience, experience of each of their scratches and stings, that is!'

She held out her hands and arms which were a mass of minor abrasions and Tim joined in her laughter.

A week later, the team was just leaving the toolshed on the way to another day of ground clearance when, hearing a shout, Jill turned and saw her brother coming round the corner on his way to join them.

'Tim!' she exclaimed as he grabbed her in a bear hug and swung her off her feet in one of his expansive greetings. Breathless, she added, 'So here you are then. Come and meet everybody. This is Tim, everybody, who has volunteered his help. Mark, Megan, Steve, Rob.'

She indicated the others who came forward with smiles and handshakes.

'Right, let's go,' Mark said as soon as the introductions were over.

Jill was surprised to see that he was the only one who had not welcomed Tim with genuine, friendly warmth. A handshake and some polite remarks, yes, but he seemed quite cool and distant, certainly not as pleased at the prospect of another pair of hands as she would have expected. How odd. What an enigmatic man this was.

Jill decided at that moment to try and find out what made him tick. After all, the other day, when he had asked each of them in turn about their private lives and motivation, he had not given away much about himself. So, Jill would stick out her neck and ask him.

Her opportunity came at lunchtime, when they all met back in the courtyard of the old stables, where a former harness-room had been cleaned out and furnished with chairs and the basic essentials for tea-making. Mark had wandered outside with a mug of tea in one hand and a sandwich in the other, and had perched on the rim of the old horse-trough which stood in the centre of the yard. After a moment or two, Jill strolled casually over to join him as if by accident and turned her face to the sun.

'Too good to stay indoors, isn't it?'

she remarked. 'Especially in that dark, little room.'

'Mm,' Mark replied through a mouthful. 'I could get used to this gipsy way of life. It certainly beats researching.' He grinned and took a swig of tea. 'The only thing is, I've got a pile of textbooks to get through before the autumn, and I'm always too tired at night to open them.'

'These are for the forestry exams, are they?' Jill enquired, biting into an apple, and Mark nodded, his face full of enthusiasm.

'Yeah. I'm doing a course over the internet, with occasional tutorials at the Duchy College. It's absorbing stuff and I'm really enjoying it. Also, it means I can work from home and don't have to give up the day job. Ideal.'

He smiled down at her.

'And where's home?' Jill went on, taking advantage of this good mood to do some probing.

But the mood changed with the question.

'I'm living with my parents at the moment, in Truro,' Mark replied then his mouth closed like a trap.

Jill's eyebrows rose in surprise at the defensiveness in his voice and the sudden coldness of his eyes. Then, without warning, he picked up his sandwich wrapper and empty mug and grunted, 'Well, I must get on. Things to do. See you back at the site.'

Jill stared at his retreating back in amazement. What had she said to bring about such a reaction? Nothing. And what had she learned? Also nothing, only that he lived with his parents, at the moment. Why at the moment? Where else did he live, or had lived?

Jill sighed and rose to her feet, but, after all, it was really none of her business.

3

It was a few days before Jill had a chance to dip into the old diary again. The team had been working overtime in order to get the initial clearance of the grounds done before the next inspection, and were now taking a day off before beginning on a new stage. They would be looking for the remains of the features that had been part of the original grounds, a more interesting job entirely, which would make a welcome change from hacking back vegetation.

Jill felt a twinge of guilt occasionally, knowing that she should have reported her find to Mark before now. It was an important, historical document, after all, and should be displayed in the house. But Jill had become so wrapped up in Celia's story that she almost felt that she knew her personally, and that to put the diary on public view was tantamount to betrayal.

I know I shall have to, eventually, she told herself, just not yet.

She was sitting at the kitchen table after supper when she reached for the diary again and turned to the page where she had left off reading the previous time and immersed herself in Celia's world.

My wishes are all coming true, Celia continued writing. *This morning, William was sent to help me with the garden and we have spent the whole day together! He said he had to try hard not to laugh when the heard gardener called him over and said, 'Right, young Martin, this may be a tedious job but someone has to do it. You're to help Lady Celia in that little patch of hers behind the walled garden.'*

Jill blinked with astonishment and the book dropped to her lap. Martin? That was her name! She clapped a hand to her mouth. William Martin had been her own great-great grandfather! And he and Celia had obviously been attracted to one another. How intriguing! Perhaps this accounted for the kind of recognition or empathy that had been tugging at her right from the time she had first found the diary, the reason why she felt that she almost knew this couple, and which made her so reluctant to share them with the others.

But in their world what, Jill wondered, could the future possibly hold for these two, the daughter of the manor and one of its gardeners. Surely it was a liaison just heading for trouble. She had been gazing out of the window for the last few moments, lost in the past. It was a lovely evening, with the sun glinting on the silver of water which was all she could see of the creek through the trees, and turning it to gold.

Jill's conscience was telling her that there were things she should be doing in her own garden, which was becoming neglected now that she had a full-time job again. The grass needed cutting, the flower-beds were full of rampaging weeds, but . . . Jill shrugged, retrieved the diary and read on.

We worked really hard all this morning. William did the digging and I picked up all the weeds and rubbish behind him and put them in the wheelbarrow. It was beautifully warm and sunny and fortunately I had brought my shady hat, else I would have been burned brown. William was working in his shirtsleeves and waistcoat and I could not but admire the strong muscles rippling in his brown arms.

I had persuaded Bessie to make me up a picnic so that I need not go back to the house, and we sat in the summerhouse together at lunchtime. William had his bottle of cold tea and a pasty which his mother had wrapped in a cloth for him. Bessie had put far too much in the basket for me to eat, so we shared that between us as well. Afterwards, we just sat on, too replete to move, and William told me how he had great hopes of being promoted to under-gardener soon. Mr Oates *thinks very highly of him, I know. I just sat looking into his dear face and loving the way his brown hair flops in just that funny way over his forehead. His broad shoulder was very close to mine and I confess that I felt a wicked longing to lean my head against it.*

There were little thrills going up and down my spine as well and at last our eyes met and William stopped talking. Then I don't know quite how it happened, but suddenly, he was holding my hand in his big, knotty one and I was leaning closer towards him, holding my breath until our lips met and we kissed! Oh, it was wonderful — the sweetest sensation ever! I wished for it never to end.

But it only lasted a second before William jumped away and started to apologise. I laid my hand across his mouth to stop him, to tell him it was all right, and that I was not upset, but he was thinking of the dangers to us both if we were discovered. He would, of course, lose his position and I would be compromised, my reputation ruined for ever. I would not care a fig for myself, but even I could not inflict such shame on Papa. He would never be able to hold up his head in Society again.

We both knew that we had loved each other for years, ever since William started work here as a scrawny little twelve-year-old boy. We are the same age, of course, and I remember how he would talk to me sometimes when I was playing in the garden with the cousins. Edward and Julian would be climbing trees somewhere and Anne and Amelia were playing dolls' tea-parties in the summerhouse. I never could stand dolls.

I would go off and prod around among the plants and the weeds, gradually learning to know one from the other. William would be weeding or doing some other dull job like scrubbing flowerpots and he would teach me the names of all the flowers and vegetables around us. It was he who *instilled in me then his own love of growing things which has never left me.*

Oh, Jill thought, raising her head, that is so romantic. How right for each other they seem. If they had only been of the same social standing it would have been a marriage made in heaven. What had happened to them? Jill buried her nose in the book again and read on avidly.

So then I said to William, 'Well, we shall just have to keep our meetings secret, won't we?' And I know I had a twinkle in my eye because he gave me that look he has when I'm being impertinent, a look which is a cross between respect and admonition.

'And how do you think we can manage that?' he said. His own face was very glum.

'Why, this shall be our special place,' I said, jumping up with excitement. 'Nobody ever comes here except me, certainly not Papa, and it's so secluded that even the servants do not have to pass this way. I shall let it be known

that it is my private retreat, that I shall do my painting here and do not wish to be disturbed. That shall be my excuse for spending long hours out here. And you, dear William, will be the gardener whose job it is to keep it tidy for me. You can talk Mr Oates into letting you do that, can't you?'

I held his gaze and slowly a smile spread across his dear face, and he replied, 'Celia, you are the most cunning and daring little baggage that ever there was! We'll do it. I do believe it will work out as you say.'

Then he swept me up in his strong arms and lifted me as if I weighed no more than a feather as he whirled me round.

'Oh my love, how I adore you!' he said, and we became quite carried away for some minutes.

Oh, if only Papa was not continually telling me that it is time I was married I should be completely happy! I know that most girls are settled by the age of nearly twenty-one, and I know, too, *that he is worried what will become of me if he should be taken. He cannot understand why I continue to refuse Rupert's proposal. He is supposed to be so suitable, but he is such a dull and boring man!* she ended that entry in her diary.

Oh, poor Celia! Jill glanced at her watch and closed the book with a sigh. To be honest, she admitted to herself that reading it had made her realise how much she was missing having someone of her own, someone to share her life with. Not that she wanted to have Max back. That had been the right decision there, but being without a partner having had one for three years took a lot of adjustment.

Jill rose to her feet. She must tear herself away and catch up with her own life or she would no longer have a job to go to either.

In the grounds of the manor house, the rough clearance work had been completed and the whole area was looking much tidier, with definite pathways to be seen leading in various directions.

'At least we can see what we're up against now,' Mark said as they gathered in the stable yard before the next day's work. 'Although I know the undergrowth is still ankle-deep, the plan is to get in there next with picks and mattocks and see if we can uncover any of the features.'

He glanced up at them from his perch on the horse-trough where the plan of the place lay spread open on his knees.

'Then when and if we can get those located, we can bring in the heavy machinery to strip the rest, and especially to dig out the lake, which will be a major operation. Today I'd like us to try and find the grotto, which should be about . . . '

He did a mental calculation and measured across the plan with a thumb.

'About two hundred metres from the back of the summerhouse.'

They set off through a stand of

mature beech trees, their huge trunks and soaring branches giving proof of their antiquity.

'These must have been part of the original woodland, planted when the manor was first built,' Jill remarked, gazing up at the new leaves.

Clad in the soft, new green of spring and with the sun shining on them as they moved against the azure sky they were a beautiful sight. Mark nodded.

'Now that the ground has been opened up, hopefully next spring there will be bluebells here again.'

'Bluebells and beech leaves, lovely,' Jill replied. 'They go together, don't they? The classic English springtime scene.'

'What does it look like exactly, this grotto?' Rob asked as he caught them up. 'Just so that I know what I'm searching for and that I'll recognise it if I find it!'

'It was a kind of cave,' Mark replied with a smile. 'It'll either be built into a bank or sunk beneath the ground so that the entrance slopes downwards. It would have been decorated inside with crystalline stones which reflected the light, and have stone benches to sit on.'

He shouldered the spade he was carrying and Meg, following behind him with Jill beside her, gave a giggle and said, 'We look just like the Seven Dwarfs with all these picks and shovels!' And she began to sing under her breath, 'Heigh-ho, heigh-ho, it's off to work we go.'

'Speak for yourself,' Jill retorted. 'I'm not vertically challenged as they call it nowadays, even if you are, shortie!'

Meg dug her playfully in the ribs with an elbow as Mark, oblivious to it all, went on, 'Grottos were a must-have thing at one time if you wanted to be in fashion. They would be lit up with candles if the family was having a party for instance, and wanted to show off to their visitors.'

'It must have looked really pretty,' Meg said, sobering up. 'And been pretty damp and cold, too, for sitting in,' Jill added, laughing.

The group had now arrived at the summerhouse, which was still half-buried in greenery, although the ground around it had been cleared like the rest.

'Right,' Mark said, going round to the back of the building, 'here we are.'

Trailers of ivy hung from what remained of the roof and an elder tree had also entangled itself among them. Mark parted the clumps of vegetation and placed his back against the wall, ready to pace out the distance between the summerhouse and where the grotto should be, while the others walked on to meet him at the other end.

Then Mark suddenly let out a yell which made Jill jump like a scared rabbit and whirl around, to see him flailing his arms in the air like a windmill. Above and around his head swarmed a buzzing mass of angry bees, rising and falling like a cloud of smoke.

'Run! It's a nest!' he cried. 'Ow, ow, they're going for me! Get off — get off me!'

He began to spring towards the group, some of the bees following in hot pursuit until at last Mark sank to the ground trying to cover his head with his hands. Jill and the others staggered back and watched in horror, trying frantically to think what to do.

Jill was the first to recover her wits. Snatching up Mark's sweater which he had discarded on a tree-stump nearby, she sprang into action, whirling it round her head to keep the bees at bay until she reached the spot where Mark was kneeling helplessly on the ground. With a final flourish overhead, she wrapped the sweater around Mark's head and neck and seized his hand, trying to draw him to his feet. By now the swarm was diminishing as they gave up the attack and gradually flew off to rejoin the rest of the hive.

'Get up!' Jill shouted and tugged at the hand. 'This way, quickly.'

Mark scrambled to his feet and ran with her guidance round the corner to relative shelter inside the summerhouse.

With a muttered oath, he sank down on to the floor among the broken slates, as Jill removed the jacket and shook it outside. When she turned round and saw the state of him, however, one hand flew to her mouth in horror.

'Oh, Mark, you poor thing,' she cried as she kneeled down beside him among the debris and took a closer look.

His arms had taken the worst of the stings, with several on his face and neck as well. He flinched as he tried to stand and Jill put a hand underneath his elbow and hauled him to his feet, where he clutched at the corner of the broken wall for support and groaned in pain.

Jill's mind was racing. To go back to the house and find the first-aid kit would take about half-an-hour. To get help via her mobile phone would probably take as long, but her own home lay just over the boundary hedge from here. It would be the quickest option.

'Look, we must get these stings seen to as soon as possible,' Jill said, looking closely at his puffy face. 'Mark, my house isn't far away. If you can manage to scramble over the hedge, we can deal with them almost right away. Do you think you could?'

Mark nodded. He winced and screwed up his eyes against the pain and Jill noticed that he was swaying on his feet, presumably from the shock. Rob, who was among the others crowding round the door, grabbed Mark's elbow and they all added their encouragement. He seemed to be in such torment that he could hardly think straight and said nothing when Jill grabbed his other arm and set off across the rough ground towards the hedge.

'We'll come as well and give you a bunk up over the hedge,' Steve said, following in their wake and beckoning the rest to follow him. They had to run to keep up with his long stride.

'Great,' Jill said over her shoulder as they reached the great earthen bank covered with vegetation which was the boundary hedge.

The others stamped a way through the waist-high nettles and brambles at the foot of it and cleared a way for Mark and Jill. Faced with dressed stone in the Cornish style, the big hedge afforded plenty of toe-holds, and with a push from behind they were soon up and over and had dropped down to the road on the other side.

'Just a few steps now. We turn down that lane on the left,' Jill said, urging Mark along and feeling in her pocket for the door key as they reached her gate. 'Here we are.'

'Thank goodness,' Mark replied through a thick lip where one of the stings had started to swell.

Jill guided him through the house and into the kitchen.

'Just sit down there for a minute and I'll get some tweezers,' she said, pulling out a wooden chair for him. 'I've got to remove those stings before we do anything else.'

Fortunately, she knew exactly where the tweezers were, in the bathroom cupboard, as was a bottle of antiseptic lotion and some cottonwool. Jill gathered up these necessities and was back in a couple of minutes.

'Right,' she said, gritting her teeth at the thought of having to hurt him, as she lied, 'You'll hardly feel this.'

She bent down to scrutinise the swellings. Mark flinched but said nothing as she applied herself to the task and got it over with as quickly as possible.

'Now for the lotion,' Jill said with relief. 'This should cool down the bumps a bit and make you feel more comfortable.'

'Comfortable?' the sardonic reply came. 'You must be joking.'

But there was a hint of wry amusement in Mark's expression as he lifted an eyebrow. Jill was dabbing at a swelling on his cheekbone. Obviously regretting what he had just said, Mark laid one hand over her free one and said, 'Seriously though, Jill, I can't thank you enough for what you've done. If you hadn't acted so quickly I'd be in even worse pain.'

Jill felt hot colour creeping up her neck, as he seemed to be in no hurry to remove the hand. In fact his grip had tightened and their eyes were inches from one another. Jill felt a sudden urge to smooth down the ruffled hair as the moment lengthened, and had to restrain herself from doing so. She also realised with annoyance that her body was beginning to respond alarmingly to this man's powerful charm. It was too soon — her emotions were still raw after her experience with Max and she was just not ready for another liaison of that kind yet.

To break the spell she said, 'Oh, it was just luck that I happened to live in the right place.'

She withdrew her hand and took a step back, putting down the dressing pad.

'How does that feel now?' she asked briskly.

'Very much better, thanks. Where did

you learn to be such an efficient first-aider?'

As Jill moved away, Mark straightened his position and leaned both elbows on the table.

'Oh, I went on a course when I was teaching,' Jill replied. 'It wasn't compulsory but it was expected of us. It did come in pretty useful at times, too.'

She moved over to the sink to wash her hands, then turned to the work-top and plugged in the kettle.

'I'll make us a cup of tea. I guess we both need one.'

'You were a teacher?' Mark's brows rose in surprise.

'Yes, in a London comprehensive.' Jill with her back to him busied herself with mugs and spoons. 'Not far from Kew, actually,' she added over her shoulder. 'I spent quite a bit of my spare time walking in the gardens, and I used to love the Palm House. It was just like being in a jungle, all hot and humid. I suppose we could have been there about the same time.'

'What made you give up teaching?'

he enquired, meeting her eyes as she turned.

Jill shrugged.

'It's a long story,' she replied with a smile.

She had no intention of confiding her life history on so short an acquaintance, even to someone as likeable as Mark.

She was trying to think of some polite way of wriggling out of relating her personal story when she turned to place Mark's mug of tea in front of him. Then she couldn't help but smile as she caught sight of his face again, although this was due more to relief after the tension of the last half-hour than because of his appearance.

'What's so funny?' Mark asked, his own lips beginning to twitch with amusement. 'I don't look as comical as all that, do I?'

'You look as if you've been in a fight and come off worst,' Jill replied. 'Here, see for yourself.'

She unhooked the mirror hanging near the back door and handed it to him with a grin.

'Good grief!' Mark looked at his reflection in astonishment. 'I see what you mean.'

He fingered the blister below his eye, which was distorting that side of his face.

'This makes me look really evil, like Long John Silver and Captain Hook rolled into one!'

They both burst out laughing together.

It was only as Jill sat down with her own tea and pushed aside a pile of newspapers and magazines which were on the end of the table, that she realised that Lady Celia's diary was among them. Her furtive attempt to push it out of sight must instead have alerted Mark's attention.

'That looks like a very old book you've got there,' he said. 'What is it? Can I see?'

He held out a hand as Jill, flustered now, clutched it tighter.

'Um — er — Mark, there's something I must explain,' she stammered, reddening. 'I should have told you, and I was going to, soon.'

'Jill, what on earth are you going on about?' Mark said. 'You're looking as guilty as if you'd been caught stealing the Crown Jewels.'

Jill gave a nervous giggle and passed the book over to him.

'I do feel guilty,' she admitted, 'because, you see, I found this in the summerhouse the other day. I know I should have told you then, but it was so fascinating because it has connections with my family, that I wanted to read it first and then it became sort of special to me and — '

'Stop!'

Mark held up a hand and halted her in mid-flow.

'Cease your babbling, woman!'

He turned the first few pages and whistled in surprise.

'A diary! Celia Carlyon!'

He raised his head and met Jill's eyes, then turned back to read one of the entries.

'Is this the Lady Celia who did the paintings?'

Jill nodded.

'Oh, Mark, it's absolutely priceless. The whole story of her young womanhood is there. And you'll never guess what.' Jill was losing all her former nervousness in her enthusiasm for the tale she was telling. 'She was having an affair with my great-great-grandfather, William Martin, the gardener! More than an affair — they were deeply in love with each other. Isn't that fantastic!'

'Wow, it's certainly interesting.'

Mark appeared as intrigued as she was as he scanned the pages briefly.

'I haven't finished reading it yet, you see,' Jill went on, 'and I wanted to get to the end before I reported finding it. You do understand, don't you Mark? You're not mad at me are you?'

She fixed anxious eyes on his bent head and waited for his reply. At last he looked up and replied with a touch of annoyance.

'Oh, for heaven's sake, Jill, what sort

of monster do you take me for? Stop looking like a school kid up before the head, and tell me how you found this.'

Jill explained about the broken drawer and also mentioned the pen and ink bottle that were with the diary.

'Celia must have kept them in the summerhouse because it was private,' she finished. 'Where she and William had their secret meeting-place. Oh, wasn't it romantic! Don't you think so?'

Mark grunted and handed the diary back to her.

'Keep this until you've finished with it,' he said. 'Then let me have it to read for myself. I won't mention it to anyone just yet.'

'Oh, Mark, thank you. I will.'

Jill heaved a sigh of relief and felt her burden of guilt melting away in the warmth of his smile.

★ ★ ★

'How's your face feeling now?' Jill asked when they met for work the next day.

'Not too bad,' Mark replied. 'Stiff, itches a bit, but the swelling's gone down a lot as you can see. I'll live, thanks to your ministrations.' He grinned. 'Just as well, with the weekend coming up. I'm doing the tour guide bit around the house tomorrow. Don't want to frighten the old ladies away with my evil leer!'

They all joined in the laughter and Mark added, looking in Jill's direction, 'By the way, as a point of interest, I've been told that the rooms which were damaged by the storm have been re-opened. You remember, Lady Celia Carlyon's bedroom and sitting-room?'

Jill's face brightened.

'Oh, yes. I must see those. I'd better come on your tour. I'll tell Tim as well. He's never been round the house and he's very interested in old buildings. Oh, there he is now,' she added as her brother appeared around the corner and waved a hand. 'I'll let him know right away, before I forget. Hi, Tim,' she said as they met, and her brother

86

greeted her with a hug as Jill stood on tiptoe to give him a peck on the cheek.

Did she imagine it or had the smile slid from Mark's face as he replied, 'Yes, of course,' and turned away to speak to one of the others.

Jill shrugged. It was of no importance.

Jill was now about halfway through Lady Celia's diary and her reading was speeding up as she had become more accustomed to deciphering the old-fashioned script. As she sat down with it later next morning there had been a huge lapse since the last entry, and it was now 1903, which was explained as Celia wrote.

At last I can get back to my journal again. I have had very little time to myself for some months, having been much occupied with Papa's illness. The influenza has been rife in and around the village. He seems much better now although it has left him very weak. Meanwhile, such a lot has happened that I hardly know how to begin. Poor,

poor Mr Oates, the head gardener, passed away during the epidemic, which is very sad as he leaves a wife and family, but, of course, we shall do all we can for them. But it means that my beloved William has been appointed in his place and I cannot help but be joyful for that!

And that is not all. For a long time Papa has been very jealous that other county families like ours are acquiring exotic plants from all over the world for their gardens and glasshouses, and he does not mean to be left out in this current fashion. He says it is all very well to be given cuttings and seeds by other people, but he would like to find some rarity that he could introduce as his own discovery. So, he has asked William to go abroad for him, possibly to the jungles of Brazil, to search out unknown species for him! It is so exciting, but I cannot bear to think of William being away for such a long time. How I long to go, too, but that can never be, as I am a young lady.

So deep in Celia's life was she that Jill could almost hear the sigh which accompanied that last remark and imagined the other girl, her chin resting on her hand, looking longingly out of the window of the summerhouse, perhaps seeing the same beech trees that Jill had done, but imagining the jungles of the Amazon.

Jill came back to earth with a start and glanced at the clock. So late! She would miss the tour of the house if she didn't get a move on. She abandoned the diary for the time being, threw together a hasty lunch then ran up the road to the manor.

Jill arrived just as the group was filing in through the entrance. She saw Tim looking back anxiously over his shoulder, obviously wondering where she was.

'Phew. Just made it!' she exclaimed, smoothing a hand over her rumpled hair. 'I lost all track of the time.'

'Thought you'd changed your mind,' her brother replied, digging into a pocket for loose change. 'I'll get these,' he added as they passed the ticket desk.

'Oh, thanks, I'll do the same for you sometime,' Jill replied, looking around her at the selection of tourist advertising material on display. 'Actually, I want a copy of the guide book for myself, and I must have that history of the Carlyon family,' she muttered under her breath, hoping that Tim was not going to ask why.

His back was towards her as he was talking to the woman over the counter and he hadn't heard her. Jill hastily paid for her purchases and stuffed them into her shoulder bag, then followed in her brother's wake to the far side of the hall.

There was a larger party here today, presumably due to the holiday season which usually started around Easter. Surprisingly, there was no sign of Mark yet. Jill glanced at her watch and noticed it was past time for the tour to begin. A few minutes passed and some of the other people who had been wandering around the hall gazing at the family portraits rejoined the group and began murmuring and shuffling their feet.

At last there was a screech of brakes as a car drew up outside and Mark came running up the steps.

'I'm so sorry to have kept you waiting, ladies and gentlemen,' he announced. 'My sincere apologies for the delay, but I had to take my wife into Falmouth and I got caught up in traffic on the way back. Now if you'll follow me, please.'

4

It was inevitable, of course. That such an attractive man of Mark's age should be single was highly unlikely after all, but Jill had thought, probably only because she was lonely herself, that . . . and he didn't wear a ring because she'd looked, but then not all men did. But why hadn't he mentioned it before?

Jill bit her lip as she trudged after the others, lost in her thoughts. Mark had said that he was living with his parents, and, like a fool, she had jumped to the wrong conclusion. He had obviously meant that they were doing so, he and his wife, and that could be for any number of reasons. They could be trying to find a house of their own . . . the shared house was a large one and was split between them . . . the parents could be frail and needed someone there . . . Oh, shut up, Jill told herself fiercely and tried to concentrate on what was going on around her.

They were on the way upstairs now, and Mark was indicating the bedrooms.

'And this is the suite that used to belong to Lady Celia Carlyon, the last daughter of the family. She never married and the line died out after her death.'

Mark smiled and met Jill's eyes with such a look of secret complicity that her heart turned over, but after a brief smile in return, she deliberately broke the eye contact and moved on to gaze avidly around the pretty bedroom. William Morris wallpaper with a pattern of birds and strawberries looked so pretty, along with the red and cream striped brocade spread on the brass-knobbed bed. Strawberry-red silk curtains faded into stripes at the bay window which looked out over the terrace and lawns.

'Her portrait is hanging there above the fireplace,' Mark was saying as he pointed a finger.

Jill took a step out of the crowd to move nearer, gazing up at the bright, intelligent face. Dark eyes beneath delicately-arched brows sparkled with vivacity. Celia's hair, dark and lustrous, was coiled into a chignon low on her neck. Several wisps had escaped the pins and were drifting about the lace fichu at her throat. One hand rested on a small table where lay an artist's palette and some brushes, and she was half-turned as if the painter had interrupted her at work.

It was a beautifully-executed portrait, in which the artist seemed to have captured the very essence of the lively, spirited girl that Jill imagined she already knew. She felt so privileged to have stumbled upon the story of this young woman's secret love that she was overcome with emotion and had to swallow down the lump in her throat. Mark's voice broke into her thoughts.

'And this would have been her boudoir.'

Mark and the others had moved

through the arched doorway into the next chamber. It was a light and pretty room, very feminine, and it was easy to imagine Celia in here, reading. There were bookshelves lining one of the alcoves, but Jill could also see her sewing at the little round table in the window. She glanced at some of the book titles as they passed through, and smiled as she noticed Gardening For Ladies, The Language Of Flowers, and The Gentlewoman's Guide to Horticulture, in among volumes on painting in watercolours and several rows of novels.

Soon they had finished the rest of the tour and were all filing out into the sunshine again.

'Very interesting,' Tim said, stuffing the guidebook in a pocket. 'And I almost forgot to tell you this, Jill.'

She turned to wave goodbye to Mark as she linked arms with her brother and strolled down the gravel path edged with border plants which led to the carpark.

'Richard has offered me a change of job.'

Jill's brows rose. 'Oh? Richard has? I didn't know you'd even met him.'

'We were at college together,' her brother replied, 'and I was there when he came to inspect our work on the garden the other day. Anyway, he's asked me to do a survey of the plants and trees that come to light as the job progresses, so that he can catalogue what there is left. He wants to know what exactly there is remaining from the original garden. Apparently there is a record in the archives of what used to be grown here. So I said I would.'

'It sounds right up your street,' Jill replied, as they reached the field which served as a carpark.

'It'll certainly be a change from pulling out brambles.' Tim grinned as he opened the car door. 'Look, I'll see you tomorrow. You haven't forgotten that Mum's expecting us for lunch, have you?'

Jill made a face.

'Oops, it had slipped my mind. Thanks, Tim.'

She raised a hand as he roared off towards Falmouth, where he shared a flat, then she walked the remaining short distance to her own home. The lunch visit would be a perfect opportunity for Jill to bring up something which had been at the back of her mind ever since she had discovered the diary.

She knew that in all fairness to her brother, she would have to tell him the story of Celia and their great-great grandfather, but she hesitated at going into all the details and had no intention of showing him the diary. Her brother was not the most sensitive person and Jill could not bear to think of him holding the precious love story up to ridicule of the nudge-nudge variety.

So, next day, sitting in the lounge over coffee after the traditional Sunday roast, Jill broached the subject.

'Mum, am I right in thinking that years ago, Dad researched the family tree? I believe he did it for his own side, didn't he?'

'Oh, yes, dear. After he retired it

became almost an obsession with him. He would spend hours poring over records on those microfilms that they have at the library. I think he joined some sort of family history club as well, over the internet, and there was a magazine about it that he subscribed to.'

She paused for a moment and gazed out of the window, her fingers drumming on the arm of her chair.

'I know it was good for him to have an interest like that, as his health was failing even then, but he wasn't much company for me,' Laura went on.

'Mum,' Jill interrupted, 'do you have it still, the family tree, I mean? Do you know where it is now?'

'Of course. It's still in the sideboard drawer where your father always kept it. I saved it especially for you children, but neither of you ever showed any interest before. I'll get it.'

While they were waiting, Jill said casually to Tim, 'I asked because something interesting came up at work the other day. Of course, as you know, great-great grandfather William was head gardener at Tremorran.'

Tim nodded.

'But what I only found out since I've been up there so much is that he had an affair with Lady Celia Carlyon when he was young.'

She looked her brother in the eye and waited for his reaction.

'What? With the daughter of the manor?'

Tim threw back his head and laughed.

'Good for him, I say.'

'Here it is, I put my hand on it straight away.'

Her mother came in at just the right moment for Jill. Tim did not ask any more questions and was obviously not that interested. Great! She took the scroll of paper from Laura and unrolled it, spreading it out on the floor.

The conversation turned to general chit-chat about more recent members of the family and she took the opportunity to find William Martin's name. In 1910, he had married an Emily Hocking, who had borne him six children, two boys and four girls, one of whom had been called Celia!

Jill was about halfway through the diary by now and as she picked it up from the table next morning to put it away until the next session, she found that a section of the sewn pages was so loose that, as she opened the book, it fell cleanly out of the binding. As Jill retrieved it and checked that no lasting damage had been done, she realised that here was the perfect way to keep her conscience clear, by passing the part she had already read over to Mark. She was obviously going to be some time in finishing the whole book and this would mean he wouldn't have to wait so long. Then they could reinsert the loose pages afterwards.

She slipped the detached pages carefully into a strong envelope, and put it away with the history of the Carlyon family which she hadn't had a chance to open yet either. She would suggest to Mark that he called here and picked up the other part. It was too precious to carry around with her.

The team was gathering in the stableyard when Jill arrived and Mark had just started his briefing. A great many more people were now involved with the project. As it became publicised through the media, more and more volunteer help was becoming available from people whose interest had been captured. The Trust had also applied for a substantial grant and on the strength of this had already invested in some skilled labour for the more professional jobs. All this Mark was explaining as Jill arrived.

'Right,' he was saying, 'the present state of things is that the two largest of the glasshouses are under restoration now, as is the summerhouse. Also we shall have the heavy machinery here soon to begin dredging out the lake. Now, as the diggers will be going in and out a lot for the next few days, I'd like us to concentrate on the walled garden where we shall be out of their way.'

He pointed to the area directly behind where they were standing.

'As you can see, the entrance leads off from this yard. They called that part of the grounds the productive garden because most of the produce for the house was grown there, a vitally important task. They would have had soft fruit and vegetables of all kinds in there, to supply the needs of a large family and its staff all through the year.'

Mark straightened up and turned towards the toolshed, fishing out a bunch of keys from his pocket as he went.

'The ground has already been gone over with a rotavator to loosen the soil,' he went on. 'Now we have to clear it of the loose stuff, then start digging and marking out the beds. It's a huge area,' he said with a grin, handing out the equipment. 'There's plenty of room to keep everybody busy without us getting in each other's way.'

Jill dropped off her rucksack containing her lunch and personal belongings in the outhouse which served them as a staffroom, and followed the others round the comer, pushing one of the wheelbarrows full of tools for the day.

As they spread out to tackle different areas of the garden, Jill waited to see where Mark was going to be working and made sure that they were within speaking distance of each other. Megan and a few others were not far away, and for a while the conversation hinged on general chit-chat about the project, then turned to the weather, which was becoming increasingly warmer as May turned into early June.

When they had gradually moved out of earshot, Jill leaned on her rake and turned to Mark.

'Mark, I must tell you this while it's quiet.'

He straightened up his arms full of weeds, and was heading for the wheelbarrow when he paused in his stride and turned to her with an enquiring look.

'It's about Celia's diary.'

Jill slipped off one of the stout gloves she was wearing and pushed back a stray lock of hair which had escaped its tie.

'I haven't finished it all yet, but the binding's come apart and the book has split itself into two parts, so you can have the beginning if you want to start reading it.'

His face full of interest, Mark dumped his load and came back to stand beside her.

'Oh, great, yes, I would,' he replied. 'Have you brought it with you?'

'No, I haven't. I thought maybe it's too precious to carry about, and it's in a delicate state, as I said. I wondered if you'd like to drop in and collect it sometime.'

'Sure, thanks, I'll do that, maybe after work tonight?' he added over his shoulder.

'Oh, yes, that's fine by me,' Jill replied.

★ ★ ★

Jill had been home just long enough to have had a shower and begin cooking a meal when she heard the knock at the front door. She turned down the heat under the spaghetti, went down the passage to answer it, and there was Mark on the doorstep. Her eyes widened as she took in the sheaf of flowers he was carrying.

'Hi, Jill,' he said with a smile. 'These are for you, because I never thanked you properly for the way you tended my wounds the other day. I really appreciated it.'

The expression in his charismatic eyes was soft and gentle and Jill's heart missed a beat as he came closer and placed them in her arms.

Bowled over and almost speechless with astonishment, Jill could only stammer, 'Oh — oh, thank you. I really didn't expect . . . it's very kind of you, Mark. They're absolutely beautiful.'

She buried her nose in the bouquet of lilies, with their beautiful scent.

'Mm, out of this world.' She smiled,

regaining her composure. 'Do come in,' she added, closing the door and ushering him into the sitting-room. 'I'll just get a vase and put these in water right away.'

She laid the flowers down on the coffee table, and headed towards the kitchen. To her surprise Mark followed her down the passage.

'Mm, something's smelling good,' he said as they reached the kitchen.

'Oh, it's only spaghetti bolognese,' Jill said, reaching a glass jug down from a shelf holding it under the tap.

'One of my favourites,' Mark replied, perching one hip on a corner of the pine table. 'Simple but tasty.'

'You sound like a cookery book!' Jill looked over her shoulder with a smile. 'I was late back tonight, so I thought I'd made something quick and easy.'

She turned off the tap and put down the jug as she gave the spaghetti a stir.

'I suppose you've had your main meal by now, haven't you?'

Mark shook his head. 'As a matter of

fact, no. I haven't been home yet. Richard caught me on the way out and we went for a drink and a chat about work.'

He swung a leg as he glanced out of the window and whistled a little tune under his breath. There was no way out of it. She would have to ask him to stay. If it hadn't been for the flowers, Jill thought rapidly, she wouldn't have felt so obliged, but under the circumstances, how could she refuse him?

'You're welcome to stay and share this, Mark, if you'd like to. I've made far too much for one person, but I suppose your wife's expecting you home, isn't she?'

'Er — no, not tonight.'

Jill waited for him to expand in this terse reply but he didn't.

'And I'd love to stay, if you're sure you're not just being polite.'

His eyes bored into hers and Jill was sure he had read her mind, but then his face crinkled into such a disarming smile that she couldn't help but laugh.

'As if I would!' she said jokily, and reached for two plates.

The conversation during the meal was very general, only veering towards the personal when they had almost finished. Twisting spaghetti expertly round his fork, Mark looked up and as their eyes met, he remarked, 'What a lovely cottage you have here. A bit isolated though, isn't it? Don't you mind living alone?'

That's a tricky one, Jill thought, biting her lip. It was actually taking her longer than she had anticipated to adjust from being one of a couple to one on her own, but she replied with perfect truth.

'It suits me very well at the moment. I love the countryside and it's so convenient for the job, too.'

'And what will you do when the job comes to an end?' he asked, as he finished his own meal and leaned back with folded arms.

The casual remark brought Jill up with a start, with a sudden stab of something like panic at the thought of the future, for this was only a stopgap, after all. Yes, the work would last for a long time yet, but as the restoration became more and more complete, there would be less people needed, and there was no guarantee that she would be kept on as a member of the permanent maintenance staff, even if she wanted to be. And what kind of future did she want? For the first time in her life Jill faced the fact that she just did not know, and it was not a comforting thought.

'Oh, ask me again when it does!' she said, laughing to dispel the gloom. 'Cup of coffee?'

She loaded a tray and took it back to the sitting-room where she handed Mark the first part of the diary.

'That's your section,' she said. 'I've put it in an envelope for safety.'

'Ah, thanks.'

He withdrew it from its wrapper and flicked through a few pages, dipping into it here and there as he went.

'Wow — Lady Celia was quite a feisty girl for her times, wasn't she?' he remarked, raising his head and meeting Jill's eyes.

'She certainly knew what she wanted, and how to get it,' she replied with a smile.

'I'll look forward to reading it properly, when I get time,' Mark added, as he slipped the book into a pocket. 'But we've got this important meeting coming up. That's what Richard and I were discussing tonight. It's all right if I tell you now as everybody will hear about it in the morning.'

He picked up his coffee, leaned back and crossed one leg over the other.

'Oh, a meeting?' Jill raised her brows as she joined him on the settee. 'What about?'

'Well, Richard's got a lot of bigwigs coming down from London next week to look around the place. It's all tied up with getting the grant money, you know? They want to see exactly what the project is, what the place was like when we started, and what we've done to date on the very little money that we had to begin with.'

'I see. So do we all have to be there?'

'Yes, I'm afraid so. Richard would like you to be, so we can answer specific questions from the viewpoint of those at the cutting edge, if you'll forgive the dreadful pun!' he said with a grin, and they both burst out laughing together.

When they had become serious again, Mark went on.

'The way we're thinking it will go is, first I've been pressganged into doing an introductory talk and slide show, then Richard will give them a tour, during which we shall all be bringing up the rear in case there are any questions, then back to the house for refreshments. The food will be free, and that includes for us as well! An outside caterer is seeing to that. There's to be a marquee in the yard.'

'Mm. Quite an occasion then.' Jill was deep in thought.

'It certainly is. The Press has been

invited. The more publicity the better, and rumour has it that TV cameras may possibly be there as well. I know I shall be thankful when my part's finished. I don't enjoy being the centre of attention one bit.'

'Well, at least you'll get it all over and done with at the beginning,' Jill replied.

Mark nodded. 'That's the only good thing about it,' he said then drained his cup, replaced it on the tray and glanced at his watch. 'Time for me to be going,' he said as he uncurled his long legs and rose to his feet.

'Well, if you're sure,' Jill said, joining him as he moved towards the door.

'I am. I've got a speech to prepare!' Mark made a face. 'Thanks, Jill, for the meal. I really enjoyed it.'

His eyes held hers for a long minute as they reached the front door.

'Right, I'll see you in the morning, then,' he added and was on his way.

''Bye, Mark.' Jill waved him off then returned, deep in her own thoughts, to collect the tea-tray.

The following week seemed to fly as they prepared the grounds for the inspection. The whole area was showing more signs of cohesion now that the clearance work was done, and the present emphasis was on cleaning up the paths and restoring the various structures as far as possible to show what they would have looked like originally.

Richard had been round several times to watch them at work, and both he and Mark had been decidedly edgy all week. The team was left in no doubt as to the seriousness and importance of the forthcoming visit. The atmosphere had rubbed off on them, too, and they were all going about their work in a more subdued fashion than usual.

By the eve of the inspection, the whole place had been tidied up and was ready. They had all been given the following morning off to compensate for the late evening ahead of them the next day, and they dispersed with a collective sigh of relief that it would soon be all over and they could get back to normal again. Jill was on her way out of the gate when she heard her name being called and turned to see Mark running after her waving a hand as he came.

'Jill,' he called, 'wait just a minute, please. I want a word with you.'

He drew to a halt, slightly out of breath.

'Sorry, I meant to catch you before you went. I was wondering if you would do me a slight favour.'

Jill raised her head and replied, 'Gladly, if I can. What is it?'

'Well, it's like this. I've borrowed a slide projector from a mate of mine, to illustrate the talk tomorrow night, and I wondered if I could possibly leave it at your house for safety. Would you mind?'

Mark gave her a searching look.

'Oh, I see. That's no problem.'

'I don't want to leave it at Tremorran,' Mark explained, 'because there'll be strangers milling about all over the place. He doesn't like lending it at all really, but I promised him I'd take great care of it, you see, and I can't think what else to do with it. Your place is so nearby that it seemed to be the answer.'

'As I said, it's no problem. Have you got it yet?' Jill asked.

'Yes, I've just picked it up. It's still in the car. May I drop it round to you now?'

'Sure. I'll get back and open the front door. See you in a minute.'

She headed off for the cottage, and was soon answering the door to Mark.

'Will you stay for a cup of tea?' Jill enquired as he appeared in the doorway. 'I've got the kettle on.'

'Oh, no, no thanks, Jill. I've still got a lot to do this evening. Look, I won't come in at all if you don't mind. I'll just put this down somewhere.'

He indicated the box he was carrying.

'In here,' Jill said, leading the way into the sitting-room. 'Put it in that corner. It'll be quite safe there.'

'Thanks, I really am grateful. I feel

bad about dumping this and running off, but you do understand, don't you?'

'Of course I do, and try not to worry,' she said with a smile. 'I'm sure everything will be fine.'

'Hope you're right,' Mark replied and was on his way. 'See you tomorrow then,' he called back over his shoulder, and vanished.

Next day, Jill was having a leisurely breakfast and enjoying the unaccustomed luxury of a weekday morning off when the imperious ringing of the phone shattered the peace. She sighed as she obediently went to answer its summons.

'Jill, it's Tim. Listen.'

'Hi, there, brother,' Jill said through a mouthful of toast. 'How . . . '

'Listen to me.' Tim's voice was urgent. 'Something awful's happened. It's Mum!'

Jill swallowed too soon and the hard lump stuck in her throat as she croaked, 'Mum? What about her? What's happened?'

'Get over here as soon as you can, Jill. I think she's very sick. The doctor's been and we're waiting for an ambulance. I'll tell you the details when you get here.'

Jill put down the phone and felt all the blood draining from her face. Mum! But she was never ill. She slung some things into a bag, picked up the car keys and was out of the house in seconds.

The ambulance was already standing in the drive when she arrived at the bungalow, and the two men were at the moment wheeling her mother out on a stretcher. Jill ran across the road and bent over the still form between them. Laura's eyes were closed and her face was an alarming shade of pasty grey.

'Mum, it's Jill. Can you hear me?' she murmured, pressing her mother's hand as the men paused to pull down the steps of the ambulance.

Laura's eyelids fluttered but did not open. There was no other response and one of the men said in a reassuring tone, 'Don't worry, miss, she'll soon be in the right place, with all the experts looking after her.'

'Oh, Tim!'

Jill's lip trembled as she turned to her brother who was standing behind her, and he put an arm around her shoulders. As the ambulance pulled away, he drew her into the house.

'We'll follow them in a minute, but come inside and close the door before all the neighbours come flocking round.'

Jill perched uneasily on a kitchen chair, so weak at the knees she could hardly stand.

'Now, tell me from the beginning what happened.'

She clutched at Tim's hand and turned to him with frightened eyes. Tim propped himself against the table and started.

'I was here, staying overnight because she had a job she's been wanting me to do for ages, putting up a new curtain rail. Thank goodness I was here, because early this morning, when I woke up, I could hear her moving around in the bathroom, but I didn't think anything of it. Then though, there was this almighty crash, followed by complete silence. So I got out of bed and knocked on the bathroom door to ask if she was all right, but there was no reply. I was getting really worried by then, and tried the door. Fortunately, she hadn't locked it and I went in, and there she was, slumped on the floor.'

Jill took a sharp breath and her hand flew to her mouth.

'She was conscious then, but looking pretty ghastly,' Tim said. 'So I tried to remember what to do. Don't move her, I thought, that's what they say. So I ran and got blankets and a pillow and made her as comfortable as I could then phoned the doctor and he was here within minutes. He took one look at her and called the ambulance. It's either a heart attack or a stroke, he thinks.'

Jill leaned her cheek against the back of his hand and let out all the breath she had been holding in a long sigh.

'Oh, Tim, if you hadn't been here, acted so promptly, she might have . . . '

'Yes,' Tim said briefly and straightened up. 'Now we'd better follow that ambulance to the hospital. We'll take my car. You don't look in a fit state to drive anywhere at the moment.'

Tim and Jill stayed at the hospital all that day as Laura regained consciousness and underwent a long-drawn out series of tests for various purposes. Eventually her condition was diagnosed as a severe heart attack and by late afternoon they were all allowed to see her briefly. They were told that their mother was to remain in hospital under observation for the foreseeable future, and that if she took things more easily after she had recovered, there was no reason why she would not return to her normal life.

By the time the two of them emerged at last into the evening air, the sun was going down over the western hills and staining the sky with spectacular streaks of flame and apricot. It was then that Jill's own heart missed a beat and her hand flew to her mouth in horror as she remembered what she would have been doing the day. The all-important visit had passed without her, and worse — Mark's precious slide projector was still safely stowed away in the corner of her sitting-room.

5

It was the last straw. Already worn out to the point of exhaustion by the day's events, Jill climbed wearily into bed and wondered how she was ever going to be able to face Mark in the morning. Surely he was only human, she thought, as she switched off the light. He would understand if she explained that it was an emergency and that her mother's life had been at stake. Jill pulled the duvet over herself and yawned. All she could do was apologise.

Jill was awake early the following morning and telephoned the hospital as soon as regulations allowed. She learned that Laura had spent a comfortable night and her condition was stable.

Reassured that her mother was not in any danger, Jill left for work a little early, hoping to catch Mark on his own, but he was already there and, along with several others, had started dismantling the marquee. When he saw her coming, however, he downed tools, muttered something to the man beside him and came stalking across the grass towards her.

'Mark!' Jill called out as soon as they were within speaking distance, 'Oh, Mark, I'm so sorry about yesterday.'

His face was dark with anger and his eyes were flashing sparks as they met.

'Where on earth were you?' he ground out through clenched teeth. 'The whole day — I was expecting you to turn up sometime at least, then when the evening came and there was still no sign of you or any word! What happened?'

He looked closely into Jill's face with eyes that bored into her skull like laser beams.

Unnerved by his vehemence Jill stuttered, 'I was called away . . . at a minute's notice. Tim phoned and we spent the day in Truro. There was no way I . . .'

'Jill, how could you?' His voice was deadly calm but his expression of contempt spoke louder than words. 'I trusted you. You knew how important yesterday was to me, especially the evening.' He paused and gave her a searching look. 'And when I called round, the house was locked up and there was no sign of life.' He spread his hands. 'And you didn't even phone, leave a message, nothing.'

'I've said I'm sorry, Mark,' Jill repeated in a small voice. 'It was an emergency, you see . . . and Tim . . . '

Mark had turned on his heel and was pacing back and forth, his hands stuffed in his pockets.

'So I had to stand there like a fool, apologising because there were no slides.' He scowled. 'The very thing we needed most to make an impact was the visual images. They were supposed to underscore the whole meaning of the talk.' He stopped and met her eyes once more as he added, 'Jill, I thought more of you than that. I never imagined for one moment that you would let me down.'

He dropped his gaze and scuffed the toe of his trainer in the grass. When he raised his head again his expression was furious.

'But your boyfriend only has to lift his little finger and you go swanning off for the day without another thought in your head!'

Fury had stiffened Jill's body now and her eyes were blazing as she raised her chin and countered him head on.

'It wasn't like that,' she spat out, then stamping her foot in frustration she added, 'And if you would only listen to me, I told you this was urgent.'

'Don't talk to me about urgent,' Mark replied with sarcasm. 'I think I've had some experience of urgent myself.'

He broke off and looked over his shoulder as a voice called his name.

'I have to go,' he said tersely. 'Perhaps it would be best if we kept out of each other's way for the rest of the day.'

He turned his back and strode away.

Jill's head was reeling and she was furiously angry, chiefly from the unfairness of it all. He had hardly let her get a word in edgeways, much less explain her own side of the story. Bursting with frustration, her hands clenched into fists at her sides, she turned down the path which led to the walled garden where the others would be working. Then suddenly Jill stopped in her tracks as something which Mark had said actually penetrated her brain. He had called Tim her boyfriend!

Jill jerked out of her reverie and put a hand to her mouth as her fury dissipated and her eyes began to sparkle. How Mark had come to make such a monumental mistake she had no idea, but somehow she didn't feel quite as low as she had a few moments ago. In fact, she gave a little chuckle as she reached the gate of the garden and picked up a wheelbarrow full of rubbish which she began to trundle towards the dump.

'So how did the big day go, Meg?'

she enquired as she joined her friend who was on her knees, weeding one of the side beds at the foot of the wall.

'Oh, hi, Jill.' The other girl looked over her shoulder. 'Very successful, I guess, but where were you? I didn't see you all day.'

Jill explained the situation, finishing by saying, 'So Mark's seething, of course, and we're not on speaking terms at the moment.'

'Oh, he'll soon get over it,' Meg said unperturbed. 'His speech sounded all right to me, even without the slides. And they all had loads of printed handouts to take away with them. What they don't know about, they can't miss, I say.'

Cheered by her friend's practicality, Jill reached for a trowel and began to work at the other end of the bed, still near enough to chat companionably, but where they would not be in each other's way.

After leaving work, Jill sped up to the hospital to visit Laura, who was sitting up in bed looking almost her normal self.

'Oh, Mum,' she said, bending down to kiss her on the cheek, 'you gave us such a fright yesterday! Don't ever do that again!'

Laura smiled.

'I'll certainly try not to,' she said. 'The nice doctor here has given me some medication which I have to take, and he says I must slow down and not do so much in future.'

'Quite right,' Jill agreed. 'Now, you make sure you do exactly as you're told, and start putting yourself first for once. This has come as a warning that you've been overdoing things. It's time to stop running around after all these good causes of yours and let other people take over.'

The conversation turned to general matters and Jill took the opportunity to leave when some of Laura's friends appeared at her bedside.

Back at home that evening, Jill had just reached for Celia's diary, about to get back to her story at last, when the phone interrupted her.

'Louise, hi! How are you?'

Her friend returned the greeting.

'Yes, fine, thanks,' Jill replied. 'I really am. I did make the right decision, the fresh air and exercise have been like a tonic. I feel loads better.'

She smiled, appreciating the concern in her friend's voice.

'How about coming down again soon? Your half-term break must be coming up this month. Next week, is it? Can you manage a few days? You'd be amazed at what we've done in the grounds, and I've got such a lot to tell you. You can? Brilliant!' Jill's face brightened. 'Only for a couple of days? Well, that's better than not at all. Looking forward to seeing you. We'll talk again before then. 'Bye, Louise.'

Jill replaced the receiver. It would be lovely to have Louise visit again, if only for a fleeting visit. She sank into an armchair and was soon deep in Celia's world once more. But this time the tone of the writing was entirely different from what Jill had become used to. The bright and lively spirit of the girl to whom she had felt so close had departed and instead, a dark and sombre note appeared on these pages.

I cannot believe how all my former joy has deserted me and how in such a short time I could be plunged so completely into this life of misery, Jill read. *Almost a year has passed since the outbreak of influenza and Papa is still so weak that I fear for him whenever he catches so much as a cold. But I feel for myself even more, selfish though it makes me, for I have fared as badly, if not worse. The cough which I contracted when I was nursing him has never gone away, and I have become so listless recently that it has been an effort even to walk in my beautiful garden. Working in it is out of the question.*

I have even lost my beloved William as his quest for rare plants has taken him to the other side of the world, so my plot is looking neglected and unloved, like me.

Oh, poor Celia, Jill thought, and read on avidly.

More alarming, however, is the fact that during the last few days I have been finding spots of blood on my handkerchief when I cough, and Dr Laity will not tell me outright what is wrong, although I am fairly sure I know. I have heard too much about poor Mama's last illness not to recognise the same symptoms in myself.

Jill's head jerked up and her eyes widened. Consumption, or nowadays, tuberculosis! Jill put the diary aside for a moment and reached for the history of the Carlyon family which she had bought up at the house. Celia had died young, she knew that much from Mark's guided tour, but how young? She rifled through the pages, and came on the entry Lady Celia Carlyon, the last of the family, had died in 1905.

Snatching up the diary, Jill looked at the heading. Celia had been writing this in 1904. Jill's face was sombre as she realised that as she wrote, this young woman had only a year left to live. Jill did a swift calculation. Celia had said she was the same age as William, and William had been born in 1880. To die at twenty-five! How tragic. Jill felt a catch in her throat and tears burned behind her eyes, for she was twenty-five herself.

She put the diary to one side, too upset to read any more that night. Rifling through the remaining pages, she realised that there was very little left. One more session would probably finish it.

As they went about their work for the next few days, Jill and Mark avoided each other as much as possible and spoke only when it was strictly necessary. He had called briefly at her home to collect the projector, but had not come inside the house and conversation had been kept to a bare minimum. At work it was not difficult to keep out of each other's way as the grounds covered such a large area, and the team was broken into smaller groups now and spread around the place, each one concerned with a specific task.

★ ★ ★

'Certain parts of the grounds are open to the public as well now, so I'll be able to give you a proper tour,' Jill said to her friend over a late breakfast.

Louise had arrived the previous evening and they had stayed up late catching up on all their news. Jill had also shown her friend the part-diary and given her the gist of what was in the other piece, which of course, Mark still had. Now they were planning how to get the most out of their short time together.

'I suppose the management wants to make as much money as it can to keep pace with the expense,' Louise replied through a mouthful of toast. 'It must be costing thousands of pounds for all this restoration work.'

Jill nodded. 'They've applied for a grant,' she said briefly, 'but we're still waiting for it to go through.'

She rose to her feet and began to clear the table. Half an hour later, they were strolling along the more distant tracks of the cleared woodland. A boardwalk had been erected around the newly-drained lake and some water-lilies were already in flower, their waxy petals floating on the still water.

'They look so perfect they could almost be artificial,' Louise said, leaning over the rustic bridge that spanned the stream.

The morning soon flew by as Louise admired the rest of the features, and the two girls spent a long time in the summerhouse where Louise listened entranced as Jill related the whole story of Lady Celia and her long-lost love.

'So we must go on the house tour this afternoon and I'll show you her rooms,' Jill said, glancing at her watch. 'Come on, let's go home and get some lunch or we'll be too late for it.'

They had joined the rest of the crowd who were gathered in the entrance when Mark arrived. Jill had said nothing to Louise about the rift between herself and Mark, her hurt had gone too deep for that, and she flinched as her friend called out in friendly fashion.

'Oh, hello, Mark. You're still doing the tour guiding, then? You must know it off by heart by now.'

He was, of course, forced to answer her politely. He glanced briefly at Jill and his face was expressionless, before he replied.

'Oh, hello — um — Louise, isn't it? Yes, that's right.' He glanced at his watch. 'We'll be moving off very soon now. I have to wait for a minimum of ten people to turn up, otherwise it's not viable, you see.'

He gave her a smile which did not reach his eyes, detached himself and moved a short distance away. As they stayed where they were, Louise turned to Jill.

'I've been meaning to ask how your mum is now. I was so sorry to hear about her heart attack,' she said.

'Oh, thanks.'

Jill, who had been daydreaming as she imagined Celia living in this house and possibly standing on this very spot, came back to the present.

'Yes, she gave Tim and me a real fright, collapsing like that. But she's home from hospital now and doing well. She just has to take things more slowly in future.'

'What's Tim doing now? He's still single, I suppose?'

'Actually, he's working on this project as well,' Jill replied. 'Cataloguing plant species for the records, and yes, he is single. Mum's always on at him to get himself a nice girl and settle down, but as you know, my brother's a confirmed old bachelor.'

Louise's voice, although not loud, was used to making itself heard right to the back of a class of noisy teenagers and it had easily carried across the hall to where Mark was standing. Jill had been looking in his direction during their conversation and had seen his shoulders stiffen. She knew instinctively that he was listening and she gave a secret smile. He could make what he liked of that, she thought, as they went forward to join the crowd which had just begun to move.

Louise returned home on the Sunday evening, with promises to keep in touch and to come down for a longer stay next time. As soon as Jill found herself on her own again she settled down to read the remaining part of Celia's diary.

I have decided that I shall paint a secret record of our love that no-one but William and I shall understand, she read. *It will be my last present to him in case — which God forbid — I am no longer here when he returns. I do feel so very weak and unwell that I must prepare myself for that eventuality as bravely as I can.*

On my better days, I sit here in the window bay of my room with the sun streaming in through the green silk curtains, and look out over the parkland and flower-beds, down towards the summerhouse. I can just see the roof of it peeping through the trees, so as I paint I think of the happy times we spent there together, and it cheers me. I miss my William so much. We cannot even exchange letters to each other and I have no idea how long it will be before he returns. He has sent a consignment of seeds back to Papa so he is well, but now he is forging ahead into deeper jungle to look for orchids and I fear for him in such dangerous terrain.

Jill raised her head, riven with the sadness that seeped from the ancient pages. Her eyes rested on the far side of the creek, where quiet fields lay basking in the evening sunshine and thought that Celia would have recognised that view, had probably walked those paths herself. It made her feel so near, and so real. She rubbed a hand across her eyes and continued reading.

Yesterday I completed the spray of

purple lilac, the first of my special flowers for William. I was so delighted with the result that it gave me strength to begin on the roses, which were also very pleasing, and I stayed far too long in one position and became cramped before I realised it. When I came to get up, my limbs were so weak that I almost fell, and I have had to spend two days in bed in order to recover. Oh, this wretched illness! There is so much I want to accomplish before ... but I must not dwell on that.

I am better again, well enough today in fact to take my painting things down to the summerhouse. Papa came with me and he sat admiring the roses while I worked. Of course he does not know the object of the flowers I am so busy with, but he appreciates them for themselves. I have now completed both the heather and the clover, being careful not to sit for too long at a time, and getting one of the servants to carry my equipment. Only two more and the set will be complete! Please God, send me the stamina I need to finish off just the rosemary and the forget-me-nots, then I will take to my bed with a lighter heart, if that is what I have to do.

Jill rubbed her eyes, which were beginning to feel the strain of peering at the faded handwriting, and glanced at the rest of the pages. They were blank and her heart fell. She had come to the end of Celia's diary at last. Jill let it fall to her lap with a sigh of disappointment, for it was like saying goodbye to a dear friend and knowing that they would never see each other again.

Jill sat for a while in a dream, the book still resting in her lap, until she was roused from her reverie by a knock at the front door. Still in a half-daze, she went to answer it and to her astonishment discovered Mark standing on her doorstep.

'Oh — um — Mark!' She stared at him, momentarily lost for words.

'Hello, Jill,' he said. 'I hope I'm not disturbing you. I'd like to come in for a moment, if I may. There's something I need to talk to you about.'

His manner was quiet, polite and totally lacking the fire and thunder of their last real conversation.

Totally nonplussed, Jill took a step back and opened the door more fully.

'Oh, right,' she said, 'come on in.'

Jill following him into the sitting-room, half-wishing that she had changed into something smarter than jogging bottoms and a baggy shirt. But it didn't really matter. Why should it?

'I've finished reading this,' Mark said as they sat down, and he produced the part of Celia's diary which he had borrowed. 'Isn't it fascinating?'

His former sober expression had given way to something more animated as he leaned forward with his elbows on his knees and looked Jill in the face.

'As a social record of the times, it's absolutely priceless. It'll make a fantastic exhibit up at Tremorran. I thought we could display it under glass in Lady Celia's room and perhaps photocopy the text and hang it on the wall beside her portrait. What do you think?'

Jill lowered her eyes to her lap and paused.

'Well,' she said slowly, 'it's not up to me, of course, as it's not mine, but I think when you've read the other part you might think differently.'

'Oh?' Mark's brows rose. 'Why's that?'

Jill looked up at him and met his eyes.

'Oh, Mark,' she said, 'it's so sad. Celia gets ill, and she knew she was going to die. She was only twenty-five. She poured her heart out in that diary and when I was reading it I felt that she was actually talking to me. It made it very special.'

Jill shrugged and looked down at her clasped hands as she went on.

'I know it sounds potty but I wouldn't really feel happy if her grief was pasted up on the wall for everyone to see, but see what you think yourself when you've read the rest of it.'

'It certainly seems to have made a big

impression on you,' he replied, as she handed him the other part of the diary. 'Maybe I'll have to do a re-think, but Richard and the rest of the management will have the last word, of course. I can only advise.'

'Yes, I do realise that,' Jill said. 'Cup of coffee?'

She rose to her feet.

'Um, in a minute,' Mark said. 'Thanks, but there's something I've got to say to you first, Jill. It's the real reason why I came round tonight. The diary was just an excuse. Actually I came to apologise to you.'

'Apologise?' Jill said in astonishment. 'For what?'

'For my appalling behaviour the other morning when I yelled at you so, and . . . and . . . '

Mark's face reddened and he looked uncomfortable. He's actually feeling embarrassed, Jill thought, wide-eyed.

'You see, I was talking to Meg and she told me all about your mother's collapse, and how you had to spend that day at the hospital. Then I remembered the way I blew my top and never gave you a chance to explain, or to put your side of the case at all.' He paused then looked up into her face. 'Oh, Jill, I am so sorry. I was an arrogant, selfish brute. Can you ever forgive me?' he pleaded.

The expression on his face would have melted a heart of stone. Jill looked back into those intense, dark eyes and was lost. She would have forgiven him anything, would have walked barefoot on hot coals if he'd asked her. But deep inside her some little imp of mischief would not let him off the hook that easily.

'Well, I was very upset at the time, Mark, I can't deny it.' Jill held his gaze. 'To think that you believed that I would let you down. That's what hurt the most.'

She paused, savouring the moment, watching him cringe. Then she asked herself, why am I behaving like this? A small, inner voice replied, Because you are besotted with him and you know he can never be for you.

The revelation hit her like a slap in the face, for it was true. She had been attracted to this man from the first time she had set eyes on him, but had not realised it until now. To give herself a chance to recover her composure, Jill rose to her feet.

'But of course I forgive you, if it makes you feel better,' she said lightly. 'It's all just so much water under the bridge now.' She shrugged. 'I'll go and make that coffee.'

She turned on her heel and left the room.

Over coffee, the conversation revolved around generalities and when they had finished, Mark rose to leave. It was as they were parting at the front door, he turned to Jill and said in a casual tone, 'How would it be if I take you out to dinner tomorrow night, just to show there are no hard feelings?'

Jill, completely taken aback, could only stare at him for a moment as she took this in.

'Oh! Well, yes, that would be lovely,' she replied.

With her mind in turmoil, she was wondering what seemed so odd about this invitation. Then she remembered. Mark was a married man!

'Won't your — er — wife mind?' she said in a small voice.

'Ah, no,' he said with a face like granite, and went before Jill could say anything more.

6

As Jill flew up the stairs to shower and change the following evening, she was wondering what to wear. She spent most of her time in working gear and this was the first opportunity she had had to dress smartly for a very long time. Eventually, she decided on a longish, floaty skirt in pastel colours, and a sky-blue top which Max had once said matched her eyes perfectly.

Max — Jill paused with the top in her hands and realised that she hardly ever thought of him at all now. In fact, she'd almost forgotten what he looked like.

As she threaded a pair of tiny silver stars through her ears and rolled on some mascara, it occurred to Jill that she had scarcely bothered with her appearance since coming back to Cornwall. It hadn't seemed to matter when she was kept so busy at

Tremorran, and she hadn't been farther than Truro for essential shopping since she had been here. She brushed her hair until it shone, dabbed on a hint of perfume and ran downstairs just in time to answer the door.

Mark was standing there, dressed in smart navy slacks and a patterned shirt in shades of cream and blue. He was also wearing a smile so wide that, as he greeted her, Jill realised that he was obviously bursting with news of some kind. It was so infectious that she immediately smiled back.

'You look like the cat that's found the cream,' she remarked. 'Have you come into a fortune or something?'

'Actually, that's more true than you realise.'

Mark stepped inside, took a deep breath.

'The grant money came through this afternoon! Jill, we've got it!'

Then his arms were suddenly around her in a big hug as he swept her off her feet and twirled her round. Dizzy and delighted, Jill could only laugh help-lessly as she looked down at the top of his head and wished that this precious moment could last for ever. But, of course, he soon set her on her feet again.

'That's fantastic news, Mark,' she said. 'Oh, I'm so glad! Not because it will keep us in work, but because it would be so awful if we couldn't finish the job after all.'

And because, she added privately, if it had been turned down, she would have had guilt feelings for ever more, just in case she'd been partly responsible.

'Right, let's go,' Mark said as they recovered their composure. 'The table's booked for eight so we'd better get a move on.'

Mark drove through Truro and on to the Malpas road that wended its way beside the River Fal, where pleasure boats rocked at their moorings and waterfowl foraged along the banks.

They ate their meal in an attractive riverside pub where it was sheltered enough to sit outside and enjoy the view. The evening sunshine was gilding the water and setting every ripple sparkling, for the tide was in, nudging at the dense woodland which sloped right down to the edge, where it gripped the river bank with huge, gnarled roots like claws.

As Jill watched, a heron flapped its way lazily upstream where its mate was standing on stilt-like legs, head hunched into its neck, waiting patiently for a catch.

'What a fantastic spot,' Jill said with feeling, as she leaned back in her chair and tipped her face up to the sun.

They ate large salmon steaks marinated in herbs and a delectable sauce, with a huge salad and an assortment of crisp bread rolls. After a dessert of local straw-berries and Cornish clotted cream, Mark slid back his chair and stretched out his long legs, leaning back with both arms behind his head.

'Oh, that was really good,' he said with a contented sigh. 'I haven't eaten this well in ages.'

'Well, it has to be better than the freezer-to-microwave lifestyle,' Jill agreed, laying down her spoon. 'It was delicious, and I'm sure I've eaten more than I should have done.'

'You're allowed to, for once,' the sleepy reply came.

Mark had closed his eyes against the sun and Jill took the opportunity to study his face. Relaxed, he looked younger than she reckoned he must be, and the air of arrogance which he sometimes put on had been replaced now by a much softer expression. What an enigma he was. He could quote poetry, loved plants, but could close up like a clam and withdraw into his shell in a second.

Since she had admitted to herself how attracted she was to this man, she had realised that the strong feelings he aroused in her were not anger or irritation or any of the negatives, as she had thought when they had had that row, but something much deeper and more sensual. It was useless of course, to think of going any further down the road.

Lost in her reverie, Jill failed to notice that Mark had opened his eyes a crack and was staring straight at her. She jumped and felt colour rise to her cheeks as he stirred and stretched.

'Well, now, how about a walk to work off all that food?' he said with a grin.

Jill forced herself out of the dream.

'Great idea,' she said lightly, reaching for her bag which was swinging from the back of her chair. 'I can see a track along by the river down there. Let's see where it goes, shall we?'

The path led them along the edge of the creek, over shingle and stones which were green with algae and seaweed. Scrubby oaks bent low over the shore, hanging almost horizontally in places, as with their exposed roots they struggled to keep their grip in the eroded soil. Clumps of dry seaweed had been blown into their lower branches and were waving in the breeze like some new variety of foliage.

Over a stile, the track began to climb upwards, skirting a field and emerging into a conifer wood. Here, the sun was veiled by the branches of tall pines and the two were walking on a springy carpet of fallen needles, the resinous scent rising in the warm air like incense. Framed by the trees, the water was intensely blue and they stopped for a moment to watch a couple of cormorants standing on a fallen log, their lustrous black wings outstretched to dry in the sun.

'This path seems to go on for ever,' Jill remarked after they'd been walking for half an hour. 'Perhaps we should turn back soon.'

She had put on a pair of smart shoes for their date, which were quite unsuitable for this terrain, and was wishing now that she'd stuck to her flatties.

'Right,' Mark said. 'I was hoping there might be a circular route, but without a map, I could be wrong. We'll go back the same way then.'

They eventually came to the stile, which was much steeper from this side. Mark climbed over first then held out a hand to help Jill, who was teetering on the top step as her wretched shoes slipped on the damp stone.

'Steady now, I've got you.'

Seeing her predicament, Mark put both hands to her waist and lifted her bodily over.

'OK?' he asked with concern.

Jill nodded, her face very close to his. Mark seemed in no hurry to release her and they regarded each other for a long minute. It was so quiet that she heard a fish pop to the surface of the water and in the bushes nearby a blackbird was singing its heart out, not a bit disturbed by their presence. Jill swayed towards him and closed her eyes against the sun as she waited for what? Of course, he only stepped briskly away from her and said, 'Good,' before turning his back and leading the way down the remainder of the narrow path towards the car.

They drove home in virtual silence, broken only by a few pleasantries, each seemingly deep in thoughts of their own. When they pulled up outside Jill's house, she turned to him.

'That was wonderful, Mark. Thanks for everything,' she said with sincerity, and opened the car door. 'Would you like to come in for a drink?' she added.

Mark consulted his watch and shook his head.

'Thanks, but, no thanks,' he replied. 'Actually, I have to go away for a few days on a personal matter, and I'm leaving in the morning. I must put a few things together and sort myself out before then.'

He looked up at her as he prepared to close her door and added, 'I enjoyed our evening, too. I'll see you when I get back.'

As Jill trudged up the path to her front door, she felt as if a shadow had come across the sun to spoil the end of the lovely day. Mark gave a wave and a smile and drove away.

It was late, but Jill was too emotionally stirred up to be able to sleep. She needed to unwind first, so she kicked off her shoes, curled up on the settee and reached for the book of the Carlyon's family history, which was nearby. She almost knew it off by heart, so often had she looked through it, but she wanted to check on a date. When did Celia's father actually die? If she had been the last of the line and had died herself in 1905, it must have been soon after she finished writing her diary. Jill skimmed the pages. Ah, there it was, yes, December 1904.

Jill gazed unseeingly out at the darkening sky. Poor Celia! The death of her father whom she adored must have hit her hard, especially considering she was mortally ill herself. Maybe it exacerbated her own condition. No-one would ever know now, but it would explain why the diary entries had finished so abruptly.

As Jill flicked through the book, her

attention was drawn again to the passage about the so-called mystery which was supposed to be attached to the flower paintings, and wondered again what it could possibly be. She imagined the pictures as they were arranged on the wall at Tremorran. There was Clover, Heather, Lilac, Roses, Forget-me-nots and Rosemary. One painting for each flower, but hard as she tried, she could make no connection between them at all.

At that point, Jill gave an enormous yawn and put the book away. She must drag herself off to bed if she was to stand any chance of getting up in time for work in the morning.

She arrived at work in time to pretend to be surprised at the news that the project had been allocated the grant money that they had asked for, and to join in the celebration which followed the announcement. Richard had cracked open some bottles of wine and all the team, with the exception of Mark, joined him in drinking a toast to the successful completion of the scheme.

Balancing on a stepladder as she attacked an ancient and overgrown apple tree with a pruning saw and secateurs, Jill wondered idly what the personal matter was that had taken Mark away. It could have been his exams, she supposed, but why not say so? Although she had felt recently that she was getting to know him better, he was just so reticent about his private life that sometimes he seemed like a complete stranger.

However, he turned up again, three days later, with not a hint of where he had been or why, and slipped back into the routine of work as if he had never been absent.

This made his visit the following Saturday morning all the more surprising. Jill was on her knees, pulling weeds out of her own flowerbed for once, and when she raised her head, there he was, walking up the path towards her. She stabbed her trowel in the soil and rose to her feet, hating the fact that her knees had weakened and trying to convince herself that it was because she had been in one position for too long!

'Well, hello, there, stranger!'

Her greeting sounded forced and trite, but was the best she could manage in the circumstances.

'Hi, Jill. Taking a busman's holiday, are you?'

'You could say that. With spending so much time at Tremorran, I never seem to have time to keep my own plot in order.'

She pulled off her dirty gloves and thrust a strand of hair back from her hot face.

'It's looking lovely,' Mark said appreciatively.

Jill glanced at her watch. She would have to invite him in, but it was right on lunchtime, and there were delicious smells floating out from the kitchen, where she had a chicken casserole in the oven, so she would have to ask him to stay.

'Come on in,' she said. 'I was just about to break for lunch.'

'I brought back the rest of the diary,' Mark said as he followed her through the back door into the kitchen. 'Richard said that you had better look after it for safekeeping until they decide what to do with it.'

Jill nodded. 'Oh, all right, then.'

'And I wanted to talk to you about another matter as well.'

Mark cleared his throat and lowered his eyes as he tapped a foot on the tiled floor. Jill raised an eyebrow.

'I must just wash my hands,' she said, moving to the sink. 'Have you had your lunch yet?' she asked.

'Oh — um — no,' Mark replied. 'I didn't realise the time. I'm sorry to intrude. Yours is smelling good.'

'It's chicken casserole and there's plenty for two,' Jill said over her shoulder. 'Sit down, it's all ready.'

'Well, I don't want to impose, but if you're sure . . . '

'I am,' Jill called over her shoulder.

'Thanks. Actually, now you mention it, I'm starving.'

He gave her a disarming smile as Jill began to set out cutlery and plates, and as a couple of forks slipped from her grasp and fell to the floor, she tried to figure out what it was about this unpredictable person that made her all fingers and thumbs.

'So, how did the exams go?' she asked lightly as they began to eat.

'Exams?' he said with a puzzled expression. 'I haven't taken them yet. They're not until November.'

'Oh, I assumed that was where you'd been,' Jill said, fishing for information.

Mark put down his fork and his face was serious now.

'No-o,' he said, meeting her eyes. 'No, it was something much more personal.'

He pushed back his empty plate.

'That was delicious. Thank you. Jill, I need to explain something to you, something I've been wanting to do for a long time but couldn't.'

He lowered his gaze and fiddled with a spoon, turning it over and over.

'It's about my marriage,' he added.

Jill's brows rose. 'Oh?' was all she said and waited for him to go on.

'You may have wondered when we've been chatting why I never mentioned my wife, or my home life at all.' Mark looked briefly up at her and Jill nodded.

'Well, I . . . ' she said.

'Yes, well, the fact is that Anne-Marie and I have been separated for two years. We came to the conclusion that our marriage had broken down irretrievably and for the last few months we've been in the throes of getting a divorce.' His gaze came back to Jill's face and her heart leaped as he went on. 'It was all very painful, but at last it's been finalised. I'm a free man again. That's where I've been for the last few days.'

He leaned his elbows on the table and rested his chin on his hands.

'Oh, I didn't mean to pry,' Jill said, flustered.

Mark laid a hand on her arm. 'I wanted you to know,' he replied. 'You see, I met Anne-Marie soon after I went up to Kew to study. She's an artist and often came to the gardens to paint. We got talking one day and discovered we shared a love of plants and flowers and when she found that I was from Cornwall, she said how much she had always wanted to live there and what a special place it was for painters. It all took off from there. We began seeing each other regularly, we made plans . . . I wanted to get back here, basically. I was homesick, so we decided to get married and live with my parents while we looked for a house of our own.'

Mark sighed and spread his hands expressively.

'We hadn't allowed for the exorbitant prices of property, especially for first-home buyers, and time went on and on as we couldn't find a place we could afford. Anne-Marie began to get edgy. She never really got on with Mum, and the situation worsened, until my wife and I had a stand-up row. We both realised that we'd made a monumental mistake. Anne-Marie was a city girl through and through. Her romantic dreams of Cornwall had been unrealistic. She missed her family and friends and she had come to hate the remoteness of it.'

Mark paused for a moment and his face was bleak.

'So she decided to go back to London, and she never returned, at least not for any length of time. End of story.'

He fell silent.

'Oh, Mark, I'm so sorry,' Jill said in a small voice.

'No, don't be.' Mark roused himself and shook his head. 'It was a mistake, as I said, but it's over and done with now and I must look to the future.'

He was looking intently at her as he spoke and Jill's heart gave a little skip.

'And I've had the impression, too, that your life hasn't been exactly a bed of roses. Am I right?'

Startled, Jill remained silent.

Mark took one of her hands in his

and added, 'I've picked up bits and pieces of it over the grapevine, but I'd like to hear the full story sometime.' He paused and looked intently into her face. 'Because I think perhaps we might be able to heal each other's wounds. What do you say?'

'I'd say yes,' Jill said simply, and her soul was in her eyes. 'Oh, Mark, yes and yes.'

The moment of closeness extended well into the afternoon as they talked and talked until the last vestiges of misunderstanding between them had disappeared for ever.

Jill found it hard to sleep that night, her mind was in such a turmoil. She lay tossing and turning for a long time. Mark's face danced behind her eyelids and thoughts of their new-found intimacy chased themselves round and round her mind. Just as she was at last on the point of drifting off, something quite unconnected with that subject made her suddenly jerk wide awake again.

She had been in a half-waking, half-asleep state, her thoughts having wandered now from Mark to Celia . . . to her diary; and the flower paintings, to the mysterious secret which they were supposed to contain, and her startling revelation was so dramatic that it made Jill sit up, rub her eyes and switch on the bedside light as she tried to recall the details.

She had been in a semi-dream in which she had been wandering through Celia's sitting-room up at Tremorran. She remembered seeing the Chinese wallpaper, the green curtains, the glass-fronted bookshelves and the books themselves, the gardening books. There had been several practical how-to volumes and beside them one called The Language Of Flowers. Jill's eyes widened and her hand flew to her mouth.

'I wonder . . .' she breathed.

Her mind was working overtime now and sleep was the last thing she felt like. There had been a craze in Victorian and

Edwardian times for giving meanings to certain flowers, like rosemary for remembrance and so on. Rosemary! One of Celia's paintings was of rosemary! Jill was becoming more and more sure that her hunch was the right one.

She could hardly wait for the morning to come. It was Sunday — Mark would be doing the house tour and she could go and ask him if she could look at the book then. Jill switched off the light and again lay fidgeting until the early hours before she at last fell into an uneasy sleep.

The following morning seemed never-ending to Jill, despite having slept most of it away as she made up for her restless night. At one point, not being able to concentrate her attention on anything, she sighed, rested her elbows on the windowsill and gazed out over the garden, across the fields and woods and beyond them, to the just-visible splash of blue from the river. It was another lovely day.

Jill glanced at the hands of the clock for the umpteenth time as they made their sluggish way around the dial. She could have lunch soon. That would take up a good chunk of time, and not long after that she could go. She was planning to wait until Mark would have almost finished the tour and catch him before the caretaker locked up the house.

At last Jill was on her way and found that she had timed the moment perfectly. Mark was just leading his flock back downstairs and into the hall to disperse, when she arrived.

'Hi, Jill.' His face lit up as he caught sight of her. 'What brings you here?' Her inner excitement must have been very obvious for he added, 'Has something happened? You're looking pretty pleased with yourself.'

'Mark,' Jill said urgently as she grasped his arm and pulled him away from the crowd. 'I've had the most tremendous hunch. It's about the so-called mystery of the paintings, you know?'

She looked intently into his face as Mark looked blankly back, then as the penny must have dropped, his face cleared and he replied with interest, 'Oh, really? Tell me about it.'

'We need to go upstairs to Lady Celia's rooms. That's why I came across here, before they close up the house. There's something there that we must look at.'

She started for the stairs with Mark following in her wake, then turned on the first step to call back, 'Have you got the key to that bookcase in her sitting-room?'

Mark held out his hand in which he was holding a ringful of keys of all shapes and sizes.

'The bookcase? It should be among this lot somewhere,' he replied. 'This is the only bunch in use as far as I know.'

'Great. Come on, then.'

Jill went running ahead up the stairs.

'Where's the fire?' Mark asked, laughing, as he took the steps two at a time to catch up with her.

Jill smiled back as they reached the top, secretly revelling in this new closeness between them.

'Here we are.'

Jill kneeled on the carpet in front of the glass-fronted bookcase while Mark tried several keys before eventually finding the right one.

'Ah, got it!' he said as the lock opened.

'That's the book we need,' Jill said, carefully removing The Language Of Flowers.

Swiftly, she explained her great idea to Mark and they took the book across to the table in the window to look at it together. Jill opened it and carefully turned the pages.

'It seems to be written in alphabetical order of the flowers, good.'

'It looks as if each entry is made up of an illustration, the meaning attached to the flower and a piece of background history about it,' Mark replied. 'That's interesting.'

'Mark, can you remember what the flowers are in the painting downstairs?' Jill asked, frowning as she nibbled a thumb in concentration. 'I know one was rosemary, for remembrance, you see?' She turned the page and pointed. 'And you've shown them so often to people on the guided tours. You must know them off by heart.'

Mark shook his head.

'Sorry, no. I haven't the least idea, actually. I've always just told the story and walked on to the next thing. It's strange, but you don't always take much notice of something that you see very frequently. Have you ever found that?'

Jill, only half-listening, gave a grunt of assent and said, 'Can we borrow the book for a while? It'll be all right if you take responsibility for it, and tell whoever's in charge, won't it?'

'Yes, sure. I'll lock up the cabinet now and we'll have a look at the paintings on the way out.'

'I'll make a list of them so we don't

forget again,' Jill said as they were standing in the Long Gallery where the paintings were hanging. 'Have you got a pen? I can't find mine. Thanks. I've got some paper though.'

She was rummaging in her bag as she spoke.

'Here we are, just the thing,' she added as she pulled out a small notebook. 'Now, let's see . . . rosemary, forget-me-not, lilac, clover, heather, rose . . .'

Jill jotted down the six flowers and snapped the book shut.

There were still people wandering around as they came downstairs and she whispered to Mark, 'Let's go somewhere quiet where we sort this out in peace. I know just the place. Come on.'

'Hang on while I take the keys back and tell somebody about the book. I'll meet you outside in a tick,' he replied.

Jill was sitting on the edge of a square stone tub filled with petunias when he emerged.

'Right,' she said, rising to her feet, 'we're going to the summerhouse. OK?'

Mark nodded and they fell into step.

'Oh, doesn't it look lovely now it's all restored?' Jill sighed.

Then, brambles and nettles had covered the floor along with broken roof slates and discarded furniture. Now the roof had been replaced, the stonework power-washed until it sparkled, and the cobbled floor swept clean. The overgrown bushes outside had been clipped neatly and now framed a breathtaking view of the river.

They went inside and sat on the stone bench which ran around three sides of the interior.

'Right,' Mark said. 'Now let's see about this hunch of yours.'

Jill had opened the book and was riffling through the pages.

'Ah, heather means solitude,' she said, making a note beside her list. 'Here, Mark, you read the meanings out and I'll write them down.'

She passed him the book and sat

back with pen and paper poised.

'Forget-me-not stands for true love,' he read, 'and clover means think of me. So what?' he shrugged and turned to Jill. 'You could go on for ever like this.'

'Keep going,' Jill said with determination. 'There should be two left, rose and purple lilac.'

'Um — love and first emotions of love.'

Mark laid down the book on the seat beside him and spread his hands in bewilderment.

'Big deal. So what happens now?'

'The paintings are hung in the wrong order!'

Jill turned to him with a smile like sudden sunshine on a winter's day.

'What?' Mark frowned. 'I don't understand any of this,' he said shaking his head.

Jill, who had been scribbling away as he spoke, now put up a hand and said, 'Listen. If these were re-arranged to read, 'First emotions of love, love, solitude, think of me, true love and remembrance', would that mean anything to you?'

'Nope,' Mark said succinctly.

'Think of William's and Celia's love story, Mark,' Jill urged. 'It was an illicit love, perfect at first, then William was sent overseas and Celia realised that she was dying and would never see him again. I'm sure that this is their story in pictures. She painted these as her last gift to him. It would have been the only way she could leave a message without their affair being discovered, you see?'

She looked up into Mark's face, willing him to understand, and thrust the notebook under his nose as she pointed at the page.

'Look closely and you can see it. First emotions of love, being in love, then William goes away, so Celia is left in solitude. Then comes, think of me, my true love and after my death, remember.'

Jill turned to Mark and there were

tears in her eyes now.

'That has to be it, doesn't it? Oh, tell me I'm not wrong, Mark.'

Mark put his two arms about her shoulders and drew her to him.

'You, my own love, are the cleverest girl I have ever come across. To have worked all that out by yourself is utterly brilliant. I'm impressed.'

'I couldn't have done it if I hadn't felt so close to Celia through reading her diary,' she said dreamily. 'And do you know that, years later, William called one of his daughters Celia? I suppose she would have been some sort of relation of mine, actually.'

'What a tragic story,' Mark said as he laid his cheek against Jill's hair.

'Mm,' she replied. 'I can just imagine the two of them sitting here like we are now, young, in love and all the time knowing there could never be a future for them, even if she had lived.'

'Not quite like us then. For hopefully, we shall have a future together. That is, if you agree, my love.'

'Oh, Mark, how could I not, when I love you so much?' Jill's voice was husky with emotion as his lips came closer. 'But don't expect me to paint you any flowers to prove it!' she whispered.

The End